Acclaim for Richard Russo's

EMPIRE FALLS

"Not one wrong note. . . . Russo demonstrates a stunning ability for nailing the essentials of character and atmosphere."
—*Newsday*

"Immensely satisfying. . . . [Russo is] an unpretentious master of fictional technique whose deeper wisdom expresses itself in the distinctive fallibility, decency, humor, and grace of the indisputably, irresistibly real people he puts on the page."
—*The Boston Globe*

"The kind of big, sprawling, leisurely novel, full of subplots and vividly drawn secondary characters, that people are always complaining is an endangered species. Yet in part thanks to Russo's deft satiric touch—much of the book is laugh-out-loud funny—it never feels too slow or old-fashioned."
—*Salon*

"Russo's most assured novel yet. . . . *Empire Falls* makes you wish you'd stayed in that small town you grew up in."
—*San Francisco Chronicle*

"[Russo is] one of the best novelists around. . . . As the pace quickens and the disparate threads of the narrative draw tighter, you find yourself torn between the desire to rush ahead and the impulse to slow down."
—*The New York Times Book Review*

"That *Empire Falls* resonates so deeply is a measure of its unexpected truths. . . . Richly satisfying."
—*The Washington Post Book World*

"A rare novel, thoughtful and entertaining."
—*USA Today*

"Engaging. . . . Russo's unique talent is his way of yoking wry humor to serious sadness, and rollicking entertainment to social commentary."
—*The Plain Dealer*

Richard Russo

EMPIRE FALLS

Also by Richard Russo

Mohawk

The Risk Pool

Nobody's Fool

Straight Man

The Whore's Child and Other Stories

EMPIRE FALLS

EMPIRE FALLS

Richard Russo

Vintage Contemporaries
Vintage Books
A Division of Random House, Inc.
New York

FIRST VINTAGE CONTEMPORARIES EDITION, MAY 2002

The Library of Congress has cataloged the Knopf edition as follows:
Russo, Richard, 1949–
Empire falls : a novel / Richard Russo.—1st ed.
p. cm.

1. Restaurants—Fiction. 2. Restaurateurs—Fiction. 3. Working class—Fiction. 4. Fathers and daughters—Fiction. 5. Maine—Fiction. I. Title.
PS3568.U812 E4 2001b
813'.54—dc21   2001088568

Vintage ISBN: 0-307-27513-2

Author photograph © J. D. Sloan
Book design by Virginia Tan

www.vintagebooks.com

Printed in the United States of America
10 9 8 7 6 5 4 3 2 1

For Robert Benton

ACKNOWLEDGMENTS

As usual my debts are substantial. For space, I wish to thank Fitzpatrick's Cafe, the Camden Deli, and Jorgenson's. Thanks also to Perley Sasuclark, who told me a story I needed to hear, and to Allen Pullen at the Open Hearth, who reeducated me about restaurants. To Gary Fisketjon, who has labored over this manuscript so lovingly, I'd attempt to describe my gratitude in words, but then he'd have to edit them, and he's worked too hard already. To Nat Sobel and Judith Weber, who have been with me from the start, my love. To my wife, Barbara, who reads each book more times than anyone should have to read anything, more love. To my daughters, Emily and Kate, who have been the kind of girls, and now, young women, who have freed their father to worry about people who don't exist outside his imagination, more gratitude than I can express; this time, to Kate especially, for reminding me by means of concrete detail just how horrible high school can be, and how lucky we all are to escape more or less intact.

EMPIRE FALLS

[PROLOGUE]

OMPARED *to the Whiting mansion in town, the house Charles Beaumont Whiting built a decade after his return to Maine was modest. By every other standard of Empire Falls, where most single-family homes cost well under seventy-five thousand dollars, his was palatial, with five bedrooms, five full baths, and a detached artist's studio. C. B. Whiting had spent several formative years in old Mexico, and the house he built, appearances be damned, was a mission-style hacienda. He even had the bricks specially textured and painted tan to resemble adobe. A damn-fool house to build in central Maine, people said, though they didn't say it to him.*

Like all Whiting males, C.B. was a short man who disliked drawing attention to the fact, so the low-slung Spanish architecture suited him to a T. The furniture was of the sort used in model homes and trailers to give the impression of spaciousness; this optical illusion worked well enough except on those occasions when large people came to visit, and then the effect was that of a lavish dollhouse.

The hacienda—as C. B. Whiting always referred to it—was built on a tract of land the family had owned for several generations. The first Whitings of Dexter County had been in the logging business, and they'd gradually acquired most of the land on both sides of the Knox River so they could keep an eye on what floated by on its way to the ocean, some fifty miles to the southeast. By the time C. B. Whiting was born, Maine had been wired for electricity, and the river, dammed below Empire Falls at Fairhaven, had lost much of its primal significance. The forestry industry had moved farther north and west, and the Whiting family had branched out into textiles and paper and clothing manufacture.

Though the river was no longer required for power, part of C. B. Whiting's birthright was a vestigial belief that it was his duty to keep his eye on it, so when the time came to build his house, he selected a site just above the falls and across the Iron Bridge from Empire Falls, then a thriving community of men and women employed in the various mills and factories of the Whiting empire. Once the land was cleared and his house built, C.B. would be able to see his shirt factory and his textile mill through the trees in winter, which, in mid-Maine, was most of the year. His paper mill was located a couple miles upstream, but its large smokestack billowed plumes of smoke, sometimes white and sometimes black, that he could see from his back patio.

By moving across the river, C. B. Whiting became the first of his clan to acknowledge the virtue of establishing a distance from the people who generated their wealth. The family mansion in Empire Falls, a huge Georgian affair, built early in the previous century, offered fieldstone fireplaces in every bedroom and a formal dining room whose oak table could accommodate upwards of thirty guests beneath half a dozen glittering chandeliers that had been transported by rail from Boston. It was a house built to inspire both awe and loyalty among the Irish, Polish and Italian immigrants who came north from Boston, and among the French Canadians, who came south, all of them in search of work. The old Whiting mansion was located right in the center of town, one block from the shirt factory and two from the textile mill, built there on purpose, if you could believe it, by Whiting men who worked fourteen-hour days, walked home for their noon meal and then returned to the factory, often staying far into the night.

As a boy, C.B. had enjoyed living in the Whiting mansion. His mother complained constantly that it was old, drafty and inconvenient to the country club, to the lake house, to the highway that led south to Boston, where she preferred to shop. But with its extensive, shady grounds and its numerous oddly shaped rooms, it was a fine place to grow up in. His father, Honus Whiting, loved the place too, especially that only Whitings had ever lived there. Honus's own father, Elijah Whiting, then in his late eighties, still lived in the carriage house out back with his ill-tempered wife. Whiting men had a lot in common, including the fact that they invariably married women who made their lives a misery. C.B.'s father had fared better in this respect than most of his forebears, but still resented his wife for her low opinion of himself, of the Whiting mansion, of Empire Falls, of the entire backward state of Maine, to which she felt herself cruelly exiled from Boston. The lovely wrought iron gates and fencing that had been brought all the way from New York to mark the perimeter of the estate were to her the walls of her prison, and every time she observed this, Honus reminded her that he held the key to those gates and would let her out at any time. If she wanted to go back to Boston so damn bad, she should just do it. He said this knowing full well she wouldn't, for it was the particular curse of the Whiting men that their wives remained loyal to them out of spite.

By the time their son was born, though, Honus Whiting was beginning to understand and privately share his wife's opinion, as least as it pertained to Empire Falls. As the town mushroomed during the last half of the nineteenth century, the Whiting estate gradually was surrounded by the homes of mill workers, and of late the attitude of the people doing the surrounding seemed increasingly resentful. The Whitings had traditionally attempted to appease their employees each summer by throwing gala socials on the family grounds, but it seemed to Honus Whiting that many of the people who attended these events anymore were singularly ungrateful for the free food and drink and music, some of them regarding the mansion itself with hooded expressions that suggested their hearts wouldn't be broken if it burned to the ground.

Perhaps because of this unspoken but growing animosity, C. B. Whiting had been sent away, first to prep school, then to college. Afterward he'd spent the better part of a decade traveling, first with his mother in Europe (which was much more to that good woman's liking than Maine) and then later on his own in Mexico (which was much more to his liking than Europe, where there'd been too much to learn and appreciate). While many European men towered over him, those in Mexico were shorter, and C. B. Whiting especially admired that they were dreamers who felt no urgency about bringing their dreams to fruition. But his father, who was paying for his son's globe-trotting, finally decided his heir should return home and start contributing to the family fortune instead of squandering as much as he could south of the border. Charles Beaumont Whiting was by then in his late twenties, and his father was coming to the reluctant conclusion that his only real talent was for spending money, though the young man claimed to be painting and writing poetry as well. Time to put an end to both, at least in the old man's view. Honus Whiting was fast approaching his sixtieth birthday, and though glad he'd been able to indulge his son, he now realized he'd let it go on too long and that the boy's education in the family businesses he would one day inherit was long overdue. Honus himself had begun in the shirt factory, then moved over to the textile mill, and finally, when old Elijah had lost his mind one day and tried to kill his wife with a shovel, took over the paper mill upriver. Honus wanted his son to be prepared for the inevitable day when he, too, would lose his marbles and assault Charles's mother with whatever weapon came to hand. Europe had not improved her opinion of himself, of Empire Falls or of Maine, as he had hoped it might. In his experience people were seldom happier for having *learned what they were missing, and all Europe had done for his wife was encourage her natural inclination toward bitter and invidious comparison.*

For his part, Charles Beaumont Whiting, sent away from home as a boy when he would've preferred to stay, now had no more desire to return from Mexico than his mother had to return from Europe, but when summoned he sighed and did as he was told, much as he always had done. It wasn't as if he hadn't known that the end of his youth would arrive, taking with it his travels, his painting and his poetry. There was never any question that Whiting and Sons Enterprises would one day devolve to him, and while it occurred to him that returning to Empire Falls and taking over the family businesses might be a violation of his personal destiny as an artist, there didn't seem to be any help for it. One day, when he sensed the summons growing near, he tried to put down in words what he felt to be his own best nature and how wrong it would be to thwart his true calling. His idea was to share these thoughts with his father, but what he'd written sounded a lot like his poetry, vague and unconvincing even to him, and he ended up throwing the letter away. For one thing he wasn't sure his father, a practical man, would concede that anybody had a nature to begin with; and if you did, it was probably your duty either to deny it or to whip it into shape, show it who was boss. During his last months of freedom in Mexico, C.B. lay on the beach and argued the point with his father in his imagination, argued it over and over, losing every time, so when the summons finally came he was too worn out to resist. He returned home determined to do his best but fearing that he'd left his real self and all that he was capable of in Mexico.

What he discovered was that violating his own best nature wasn't nearly as unpleasant or difficult as he'd imagined. In fact, looking around Empire Falls, he got the distinct impression that people did it every day. And if you had to violate your destiny, doing so as a Whiting male wasn't so bad. To his surprise he also discovered that it was possible to be good at what you had little interest in, just as it had been possible to be bad at something, whether painting or poetry, that you cared about a great deal. While the shirt factory held no attraction for him, he demonstrated something like an aptitude for running it, for understanding the underlying causes of what went wrong and knowing instinctively how to fix the problem. He was also fond of his father and marveled at the little man's energy, his quick anger, his refusal to knuckle under, his conviction that he was always right, his ability to justify whatever course of action he ultimately chose. Here was a man who was either in total harmony with his nature or had beaten it into perfect submission. Charles Beaumont Whiting was never sure which, and probably it didn't matter; either way the old man was worth emulating.

Still, it was clear to C. B. Whiting that his father and grandfather had enjoyed the best of what Whiting and Sons Enterprises had to offer. The times were changing, and neither the shirt factory, nor the textile mill, nor the paper mill upriver was as profitable as all once had been. Over the last two decades there had been attempts to unionize all the factories in Dexter County, and while these efforts failed—this being Maine, not Massachusetts—even Honus Whiting agreed that keeping the unions out had proved almost as costly as letting them in would've been. The workers, slow to accept defeat, were both sullen and unproductive when they returned to their jobs.

Honus Whiting had intended, of course, for his son to take up residence in the Whiting mansion as soon as he took a wife and old Elijah saw fit to quit the earth, but a decade after C.B. abandoned Mexico, neither of these events had come to pass. C. B. Whiting, something of a ladies' man in his warm, sunny youth, seemed to lose his sex drive in frosty Maine and slipped into an unintended celibacy, though he sometimes imagined his best self still carnally frolicking in the Yucatán.

Perhaps he was frightened by the sheer prospect of matrimony, of marrying a girl he would one day want to murder.

Elijah Whiting, now nearing one hundred, had not succeeded in killing his wife with the shovel, nor had he recovered from the disappointment. The two of them still lived in the carriage house, old Elijah clinging to his misery and his bitter wife clinging to him. He seemed, the old man's doctor observed, to be dying from within, the surest sign of which was an almost biblical flatulence. He'd been turning the air green inside the carriage house for many years now, but all the tests showed that the old fossil's heart remained strong, and Honus realized it might be several years more before he could make room for his son by moving into the carriage house himself. After all, it would require a good year to air out even if the old man died tomorrow. Besides which, Honus's own wife had already made clear her intention never to move into the carriage house, and she lately had become so depressed by the idea of dying in Maine that he'd been forced to buy her a small rowhouse in Boston's Back Bay, where she claimed to have grown up, which of course was untrue. South Boston was where Honus had found her, and where he would have left her, too, if he'd had any sense. At any rate, when Charles came to him one day and announced his intention to build a house of his own and to put the river between it and Empire Falls, he understood and even approved. Only later, when the house was revealed to be a hacienda, did he fear that the boy might be writing poems again.

Not to worry. Earlier that year, C. B. Whiting had been mistaken for his father on the street, and that same evening, when he studied himself in the *mirror, he saw why. His hair was beginning to silver, and there was a certain terrier-like ferocity in his eyes that he hadn't noticed before. Of the younger man who had wanted to live and die in Mexico and dream and paint and write poetry there was now little evidence. And last spring when his father had suggested that he run not only the shirt factory but also the textile mill, instead of feeling trapped by the inevitability of the rest of his life, he found himself almost happy to be coming more completely into his birthright. Men had starting calling him C.B. instead of Charles, and he liked the sound of it.*

WHEN THE BULLDOZERS *began to clear the house site, a disturbing discovery was made. An astonishing amount of trash—mounds and mounds of it—was discovered all along the bank, some of it tangled among tree roots and branches, some of it strewn up the hillside, all the way to the top. The sheer volume of the junk was astonishing, and at first C. B. Whiting concluded that somebody, or a great many somebodies, had had the effrontery to use the property as an unofficial landfill. How many years had this outrage been going on? It made him mad enough to shoot somebody until one of the men he'd hired to clear the land pointed out that for somebody, or a great many somebodies, to use Whiting land for a dump, they would have required an access road, and there wasn't one, or at least there hadn't been until C. B. Whiting himself cut one a month earlier. While it seemed unlikely that so much junk—spent inner tubes, hubcaps, milk cartons, rusty cans, pieces of broken furniture and the like—could wash up on one spot naturally, the result of currents and eddies, there it was, so it must have. There was little alternative but to cart the trash off, which was done the same May the foundation of the house was being poured.*

Spring rains, a rising river and a bumper crop of voracious black flies delayed construction, but by late June the low frame of the sprawling hacienda was visible from across the river where C. B. Whiting kept tabs on its progress from his office on the top floor of the Whiting shirt factory. By the Fourth of July the weather had turned dry and hot, killing off the last of the black flies, and the shirtless, sunburned carpenters straddling the hacienda roof beams began to wrinkle their noses and regard one another suspiciously. What in the world was that smell?

It was C. B. Whiting himself who discovered the bloated body of a large moose decomposing in the shallows, tangled among the roots of a stand of trees that had been spared by the bulldozer that they might provide shade and privacy from anyone on the Empire Falls side of the river who might be too curious about goings-on at the hacienda. Even more amazing than this carcass was another mound of trash, which, though smaller than its carted-off predecessor, was deposited in the same exact area where a spit of land jutted out into the river and created in its lee a stagnant, mosquito- and now moose-infested pool.

The sight and smell of all this soggy, decomposing trash caused C. B. Whiting to consider the possibility that he had an enemy, and kneeling there on the bank of the river he scrolled back through his memory concerning the various men he, his father and his grandfather had managed to ruin in the natural course of business. The list was not short, but unless he'd forgotten someone, no one on it seemed the right sort. They were mostly small men of smaller means, men who might've shot him if the opportunity had presented itself—if, for instance, he'd wandered into their neighborhood tavern when they had a snoot full and happened to be armed. But this was a different quality of maliciousness. Somebody apparently believed that all the trash generated in Dexter County belonged on C. B. Whiting's doorstep, and felt sufficient conviction to collect all that garbage (no pleasant task) and transport it there.

Was the dead moose a coincidence? C.B. couldn't decide. The animal had a bullet hole in its neck, which could mean any number of things. Perhaps whoever was dumping the trash had also shot the moose and left it there on purpose. Then again, the animal could conceivably have been shot elsewhere by a poacher; in fact, an entire family of poachers, the Mintys, lived in Empire Falls. Maybe the wounded animal had attempted to cross the river, tired in the attempt, and drowned, coming to rest below the hacienda.

C. B. Whiting spent the rest of the afternoon on one knee only a few feet from the blasted moose, trying to deduce his enemy's identity. Almost immediately a paper cup floated by and lodged between the hind legs of the moose. The next hour brought a supermarket bag, an empty, bobbing Coke bottle, a rusted-out oil can, a huge tangle of monofilament fishing line and, unless he was mistaken, a human placenta. All of it got tangled up with the reeking moose. From where C. B. Whiting knelt, he could just barely see one small section of the Iron Bridge, and in the next half hour he witnessed half a dozen people, in automobiles and afoot, toss things into the river as they crossed. In his mind he counted the number of bridges spanning the Knox upstream (eight), and the number of mills and factories and sundry small businesses that backed onto the water (dozens). He knew firsthand the temptation of dumping into the river after the sun went down. Generations of Whitings had been flushing dyes and other chemicals, staining the riverbank all the way to Fairhaven, a community that could scarcely complain, given that its own textile mill had for decades exhibited an identical lack of regard for its downstream neighbors. Complaints, C.B. knew, inevitably led to accusations, accusations to publicity, publicity to investigations, investigations to litigation, litigation to expense, expense to the poorhouse.

Still, this particular dumping could not be allowed to continue. A sensible man, Charles Beaumont Whiting arrived at a sensible conclusion. At the end of a second hour spent kneeling at the river's edge, he concluded that he had an enemy all right, and it was none other than God Himself, who'd designed the damn river in such a way—narrow and swift-running upstream, widening and slowing at Empire Falls—that all manner of other people's shit became Charles Beaumont Whiting's. Worse, he imagined he understood why God had chosen this plan. He'd done it, in advance, to punish him for leaving his best self in Mexico all those years ago and, as a result, becoming somebody who could be mistaken for his father.

These were unpleasant thoughts. Perhaps, it occurred to C.B., it was impossible to have pleasant ones so close to a decomposing moose. Yet he continued to kneel there, the river's current burbling a coded message he felt he was on the verge of comprehending. In truth, today's were not the first unpleasant thoughts he'd been visited by of late. Ever since he'd decided to build the new house, his sleep had been troubled by dreams that would awaken him several times a night, and sometimes he found himself standing at the dark window of his bedroom looking out over the grounds of the Whiting mansion with no memory of waking up and crossing the room. He had the distinct impression that the dream—whatever it had been about—was still with him, though its details had fled. Had he been in urgent conversation with someone? Who?

During the day, when his mind should've been occupied by the incessant demands of two factories' day-to-day operations, he often and absentmindedly studied the blueprints of the hacienda, as if he'd forgotten some crucial element. Last month, his attention had grown so divided that he'd asked his father to come down from the paper mill to help out one day a week, just until the house was finished. Now, down by the river, his thoughts disturbed, perhaps, by the proximity of rotting moose, he began to doubt that building this new house was a good idea. The hacienda, with its adjacent artist's studio, was surely an invitation to his former self, the Charles Beaumont Whiting—Beau, his friends had called him there—he'd abandoned in Mexico. And it was this Beau, it now occurred to him, with whom he'd been conversing in all those dreams. Worse, it was for this younger, betrayed self that he was building the hacienda. He'd been telling himself that the studio would be for his son, assuming he would one day be fortunate enough to have one. This much rebellion he'd allowed himself. The studio would be his gift to the boy, an *implicit promise that no son of his would ever be forced by necessity or loyalty to betray his truest destiny. But of course, he now realized, all this was a lie. He'd wanted the studio for himself, or rather for the Charles Beaumont Whiting thought to be either dead or living a life of poetry and fornication in Mexico. Whereas he in fact was living a life of enforced duty and chastity in Empire Falls, Maine. On the heels of this stunning realization came another. The message the river had been whispering to him as he knelt there all afternoon was a single word of invitation. "Come," the water burbled, unmistakable now. "Come . . . come . . . come . . ."*

That very evening C. B. Whiting brought his father and old Elijah out to the building site. Up to this point he'd been secretive about the house without comprehending why. Now he understood. He and Honus sat his grandfather, who hadn't been out of the carriage house in a month, on a tree stump, where he instantly fell into a deep, restful, flatulent sleep, while C.B. showed his father in and around the frames and arches of the new house. Yes, he admitted, it was *going to be some damn Mexican sort of deal. The detached structure, he explained, would be a guest house, which, in fact, he'd decided that afternoon, it* would *be. The river's invitation had scared him that badly. When they finished the tour of the hacienda, C. B. Whiting took his father down to the water's edge and showed him the mound of trash, which had grown since morning, and the moose, which had ripened further. From where they stood, C.B. could see both the moose and old Elijah still asleep but rising up on one cheek every now and then from the sheer force of his gas, and while C.B. couldn't reasonably hold himself responsible for either, he felt something rise in the back of his throat that tasted like self-loathing. Still, he told himself, the occasional flavor of self-recrimination on the back of the tongue was preferable to throwing away the work of his father's and grandfather's lifetimes, and he found himself regarding both men with genuine fondness, especially his father, whom he had always loved, and whose solid, practical, confident presence could be counted on to deliver him from his present funk.*

"It's God, all right," Honus agreed, after C.B. had explained his theory about the enemy, and then they watched for a while as various pieces of detritus bobbed along in the current before coming to rest against the moose. The elder Whiting was a religious man who found God useful for explaining anything that was otherwise insoluble. "You better figure out what you're going to do about Him, too."

Honus suggested his son hire some geologists and engineers to study the problem and recommend a course of action. This turned out to be excellent advice, and the engineers, warned Whom they might be up against, proved meticulous. In addition to numerous on-site inspections, they analyzed the entire region on geological survey maps and even flew the length of the river all the way from the Canadian border to where it emptied into the Gulf of Maine. As rivers went, the Knox was one of God's poorer efforts, wide and lazy where it should have been narrow and swift, and the engineers concurred with the man who'd hired them that it was God's basic design flaw that ensured that every paper cup discarded between the border and Empire Falls would likely wash up on C. B. Whiting's future lawn. That was the bad news.

The good news was that it didn't have to be that way. Men of vision had been improving upon God's designs for the better part of two centuries, and there was no reason not to correct this one. If the Army Corps of Engineers could make the damn Mississippi run where they wanted it to, a pissant stream like the Knox could be altered at their whim. In no time they arrived at a plan. A few miles north and east of Empire Falls the river took a sharp, unreasonable turn before meandering back in the direction it had come from for several sluggish, twisting miles, much of its volume draining off into swampy lowlands north and west of town where legions of black flies bred each spring, followed by an equal number of mosquitoes in the summer. Seen from the air, the absurdity of this became clear. What water wanted to do, the engineers explained, was flow downhill by the straightest possible route. Meandering was what happened when a river's best intentions were somehow thwarted. What prevented the Knox from running straight and true was a narrow strip of land—of rock, really—referred to by the locals as the Robideaux Blight, an outcropping of rolling, hummocky ground that might have been considered picturesque if your purpose was to build a summer home on the bluff overlooking the river and not to farm it, as the land's owners had been bullheadedly attempting to do for generations. In the end, of course, rivers get their way, and eventually—say, in a few thousand years—the Knox would succeed in cutting its way through the meander.

C. B. Whiting was disinclined to wait, and he was buoyed to learn from his engineers that if the money could be found to blast a channel through the narrowest part of the Robideaux Blight, the river should be running straight and true within the calendar year, its increased velocity downstream at Whiting's Bend sufficient to bear off the vast majority of trash (including the odd moose), downstream to the dam in Fairhaven, where it belonged. In fact, C. B. Whiting's experts argued before the state in hastily convened, closed-door hearings that the Knox would be a far better river—swifter, prettier, cleaner—for all the communities along its banks. Further, with less of its volume being siphoned off into the wetlands, the state would benefit from the implicit promise that no son of his would ever be forced by necessity or loyalty to betray his truest destiny. But of course, he now realized, all this was a lie. He'd wanted the studio for himself, or rather for the Charles Beaumont Whiting thought to be either dead or living a life of poetry and fornication in Mexico. Whereas he in fact was living a life of enforced duty and chastity in Empire Falls, Maine. On the heels of this stunning realization came another. The message the river had been whispering to him as he knelt there all afternoon was a single word of invitation. "Come," the water burbled, unmistakable now. "Come . . . come . . . come . . ."

That very evening C. B. Whiting brought his father and old Elijah out to the building site. Up to this point he'd been secretive about the house without comprehending why. Now he understood. He and Honus sat his grandfather, who hadn't been out of the carriage house in a month, on a tree stump, where he instantly fell into a deep, restful, flatulent sleep, while C.B. showed his father in and around the frames and arches of the new house. Yes, he admitted, it was *going to be some damn Mexican sort of deal. The detached structure, he explained, would be a guest house, which, in fact, he'd decided that afternoon, it* would *be. The river's invitation had scared him that badly. When they finished the tour of the hacienda, C. B. Whiting took his father down to the water's edge and showed him the mound of trash, which had grown since morning, and the moose, which had ripened further. From where they stood, C.B. could see both the moose and old Elijah still asleep but rising up on one cheek every now and then from the sheer force of his gas, and while C.B. couldn't reasonably hold himself responsible for either, he felt something rise in the back of his throat that tasted like self-loathing. Still, he told himself, the occasional flavor of self-recrimination on the back of the tongue was preferable to throwing away the work of his father's and grandfather's lifetimes, and he found himself regarding both men with genuine fondness, especially his father, whom he had always loved, and whose solid, practical, confident presence could be counted on to deliver him from his present funk.*

"It's God, all right," Honus agreed, after C.B. had explained his theory about the enemy, and then they watched for a while as various pieces of detritus bobbed along in the current before coming to rest against the moose. The elder Whiting was a religious man who found God useful for explaining anything that was otherwise insoluble. "You better figure out what you're going to do about Him, too."

Honus suggested his son hire some geologists and engineers to study the problem and recommend a course of action. This turned out to be excellent advice, and the engineers, warned Whom they might be up against, proved meticulous. In addition to numerous on-site inspections, they analyzed the entire region on geological survey maps and even flew the length of the river all the way from the Canadian border to where it emptied into the Gulf of Maine. As rivers went, the Knox was one of God's poorer efforts, wide and lazy where it should have been narrow and swift, and the engineers concurred with the man who'd hired them that it was God's basic design flaw that ensured that every paper cup discarded between the border and Empire Falls would likely wash up on C. B. Whiting's future lawn. That was the bad news.

The good news was that it didn't have to be that way. Men of vision had been improving upon God's designs for the better part of two centuries, and there was no reason not to correct this one. If the Army Corps of Engineers could make the damn Mississippi run where they wanted it to, a pissant stream like the Knox could be altered at their whim. In no time they arrived at a plan. A few miles north and east of Empire Falls the river took a sharp, unreasonable turn before meandering back in the direction it had come from for several sluggish, twisting miles, much of its volume draining off into swampy lowlands north and west of town where legions of black flies bred each spring, followed by an equal number of mosquitoes in the summer. Seen from the air, the absurdity of this became clear. What water wanted to do, the engineers explained, was flow downhill by the straightest possible route. Meandering was what happened when a river's best intentions were somehow thwarted. What prevented the Knox from running straight and true was a narrow strip of land—of rock, really—referred to by the locals as the Robideaux Blight, an outcropping of rolling, hummocky ground that might have been considered picturesque if your purpose was to build a summer home on the bluff overlooking the river and not to farm it, as the land's owners had been bullheadedly attempting to do for generations. In the end, of course, rivers get their way, and eventually—say, in a few thousand years—the Knox would succeed in cutting its way through the meander.

C. B. Whiting was disinclined to wait, and he was buoyed to learn from his engineers that if the money could be found to blast a channel through the narrowest part of the Robideaux Blight, the river should be running straight and true within the calendar year, its increased velocity downstream at Whiting's Bend sufficient to bear off the vast majority of trash (including the odd moose), downstream to the dam in Fairhaven, where it belonged. In fact, C. B. Whiting's experts argued before the state in hastily convened, closed-door hearings that the Knox would be a far better river—swifter, prettier, cleaner—for all the communities along its banks. Further, with less of its volume being siphoned off into the wetlands, the state would benefit from the acquisition of several thousand acres of land that might be used for purposes other than breeding bugs. No real environmental movement in the state of Maine would exist for decades, so there was little serious opposition to the plan, though the experts did concede—their voices low and confidential now—that a livelier river might occasionally prove too lively. The Knox, like most rivers in Maine, was already prone to flooding, especially in the spring, when warm rains melted the northern snowpack too quickly.

A more practical obstacle to C. B. Whiting's alterations was that the Robideaux Blight had somehow been overlooked when previous generations of Whitings were buying up the river frontage. This parcel was owned by a family named Robideaux, whose title extended back into the previous century. But here, too, fate smiled on C. B. Whiting, for the Robideauxs turned out to be both greedy and ignorant, the precise combination called for by the present circumstance. More sophisticated people might have suspected the worth of their holdings when approached by a rich man's lawyers, but the Robideauxs apparently did not. Their primary fear seemed to be that C. B. Whiting would actually come inspect the land they were selling him, see how worthless it was for farming, the only use they'd imagined for it, and promptly back out of the deal.

Having no such intention, he purchased their acreage at what they imagined to be an extortionary price, and for years afterward they continued to believe they'd one-upped one of the richest and most powerful men in Maine, whose purchase of the Robideaux Blight just went to prove what they'd always known—that rich people weren't so damn smart. C. B. Whiting, himself again after coming out of his funk, came to a conclusion every bit as dubious: that he'd trumped not only the Robideauxs, who'd had him over a barrel and were too ignorant to suspect it, but also God, whose river he would now improve upon.

The dynamiting of the Robideaux Blight some seven miles upstream could be felt all the way to Empire Falls, and on the day in August when the blasting was complete C. B. Whiting knelt on the riverbank before his newly completed house and watched with pride as the freshly energized currents bore off what little remained of the moose, along with the ever-increasing mound of milk cartons, plastic bottles and rusted soup cans, all bobbing their way south toward an unsuspecting Fairhaven. The river no longer whispered despair as it had earlier in the summer. Reenergized, it fairly chortled with glee at his enterprise. Satisfied with the outcome, he lit a cigar, inhaled deeply of sweet summer air, and regarded the slender woman at his side, whose name, by no coincidence, was Francine Robideaux.

Francine was a bright, ambitious young woman, newly graduated from

Colby College, some ten years C. B. Whiting's junior, and until the day her family closed the deal to sell her future husband the Robideaux Blight, she'd never laid eyes on him, though of course she'd heard of him. C.B. himself had graduated from Colby, as had his father and grandfather, whereas Francine was the first Robideaux to continue her education beyond high school. Thanks to a scholarship, she had emerged from Colby no longer recognizable as a Robideaux in deportment, speech or mannerism, which disturbed and angered her family, who never would have allowed her to attend college had they known how contemptuous of them she'd be upon her return. A poor girl among rich ones, Francine Robideaux had carefully observed and then adopted their table manners, fashion sense, vocal idiosyncrasies and personal hygiene. At Colby she'd also learned to flirt.

In the soft light of his lawyers' book-lined offices, C. B. Whiting, who had not looked seriously at a woman since returning to Maine, liked the look of Francine Robideaux. He also appreciated that she was a Colby graduate and admired that she appeared to understand that he was snookering her family and didn't necessarily object. Every time he glanced at her, every time she spoke, he was more impressed, for the girl seemed able to convey, without contradiction, that she was observing him carefully, even as other of her mannerisms suggested that maybe, so far as she was concerned, he wasn't even in the room. Maybe he was there and maybe he wasn't, depending. To resolve the issue of whether he was there or not, he resolved to marry her if she would have him.

Well, as it turned out, she would. They were wed in September, leaving C. B. Whiting the rest of his days on earth to try to remember what exactly it was about the look of Francine Robideaux that had so appealed to him in the soft light of the lawyers' offices. In natural light she looked rather pinched, and in the manner of a great many women of French Canadian ancestry, she lacked a chin, as if someone had already pinched her there. He also came to understand that marrying Francine Robideaux would not answer as conclusively as he'd hoped the question of whether or not he was actually in the room. On that late afternoon in August when he lit a cigar in celebration, his wife-to-be at his side, C. B. Whiting studied his fiancée carefully. Whiting men, all of whom seemed to be born with sound business sense, each invariably gravitated, like moths to a flame, toward the one woman in the world who would regard making them utterly miserable as her life's noble endeavor, a woman who would remain bound to her husband with the same grim tenacity that bound nuns to the suffering Christ. Fully cognizant of his family history, C.B. had been understandably wary of matrimony. From time to time his father would remind him that he would have need of an heir, acquisition of several thousand acres of land that might be used for purposes other than breeding bugs. No real environmental movement in the state of Maine would exist for decades, so there was little serious opposition to the plan, though the experts did concede—their voices low and confidential now—that a livelier river might occasionally prove too lively. The Knox, like most rivers in Maine, was already prone to flooding, especially in the spring, when warm rains melted the northern snowpack too quickly.

A more practical obstacle to C. B. Whiting's alterations was that the Robideaux Blight had somehow been overlooked when previous generations of Whitings were buying up the river frontage. This parcel was owned by a family named Robideaux, whose title extended back into the previous century. But here, too, fate smiled on C. B. Whiting, for the Robideauxs turned out to be both greedy and ignorant, the precise combination called for by the present circumstance. More sophisticated people might have suspected the worth of their holdings when approached by a rich man's lawyers, but the Robideauxs apparently did not. Their primary fear seemed to be that C. B. Whiting would actually come inspect the land they were selling him, see how worthless it was for farming, the only use they'd imagined for it, and promptly back out of the deal.

Having no such intention, he purchased their acreage at what they imagined to be an extortionary price, and for years afterward they continued to believe they'd one-upped one of the richest and most powerful men in Maine, whose purchase of the Robideaux Blight just went to prove what they'd always known—that rich people weren't so damn smart. C. B. Whiting, himself again after coming out of his funk, came to a conclusion every bit as dubious: that he'd trumped not only the Robideauxs, who'd had him over a barrel and were too ignorant to suspect it, but also God, whose river he would now improve upon.

The dynamiting of the Robideaux Blight some seven miles upstream could be felt all the way to Empire Falls, and on the day in August when the blasting was complete C. B. Whiting knelt on the riverbank before his newly completed house and watched with pride as the freshly energized currents bore off what little remained of the moose, along with the ever-increasing mound of milk cartons, plastic bottles and rusted soup cans, all bobbing their way south toward an unsuspecting Fairhaven. The river no longer whispered despair as it had earlier in the summer. Reenergized, it fairly chortled with glee at his enterprise. Satisfied with the outcome, he lit a cigar, inhaled deeply of sweet summer air, and regarded the slender woman at his side, whose name, by no coincidence, was Francine Robideaux.

Francine was a bright, ambitious young woman, newly graduated from

Colby College, some ten years C. B. Whiting's junior, and until the day her family closed the deal to sell her future husband the Robideaux Blight, she'd never laid eyes on him, though of course she'd heard of him. C.B. himself had graduated from Colby, as had his father and grandfather, whereas Francine was the first Robideaux to continue her education beyond high school. Thanks to a scholarship, she had emerged from Colby no longer recognizable as a Robideaux in deportment, speech or mannerism, which disturbed and angered her family, who never would have allowed her to attend college had they known how contemptuous of them she'd be upon her return. A poor girl among rich ones, Francine Robideaux had carefully observed and then adopted their table manners, fashion sense, vocal idiosyncrasies and personal hygiene. At Colby she'd also learned to flirt.

In the soft light of his lawyers' book-lined offices, C. B. Whiting, who had not looked seriously at a woman since returning to Maine, liked the look of Francine Robideaux. He also appreciated that she was a Colby graduate and admired that she appeared to understand that he was snookering her family and didn't necessarily object. Every time he glanced at her, every time she spoke, he was more impressed, for the girl seemed able to convey, without contradiction, that she was observing him carefully, even as other of her mannerisms suggested that maybe, so far as she was concerned, he wasn't even in the room. Maybe he was there and maybe he wasn't, depending. To resolve the issue of whether he was there or not, he resolved to marry her if she would have him.

Well, as it turned out, she would. They were wed in September, leaving C. B. Whiting the rest of his days on earth to try to remember what exactly it was about the look of Francine Robideaux that had so appealed to him in the soft light of the lawyers' offices. In natural light she looked rather pinched, and in the manner of a great many women of French Canadian ancestry, she lacked a chin, as if someone had already pinched her there. He also came to understand that marrying Francine Robideaux would not answer as conclusively as he'd hoped the question of whether or not he was actually in the room. On that late afternoon in August when he lit a cigar in celebration, his wife-to-be at his side, C. B. Whiting studied his fiancée carefully. Whiting men, all of whom seemed to be born with sound business sense, each invariably gravitated, like moths to a flame, toward the one woman in the world who would regard making them utterly miserable as her life's noble endeavor, a woman who would remain bound to her husband with the same grim tenacity that bound nuns to the suffering Christ. Fully cognizant of his family history, C.B. had been understandably wary of matrimony. From time to time his father would remind him that he would have need of an heir, *but then C.B. regarded his father and grandfather and wasn't so sure. Why not put an end to the awful cycle of misery right there? What was the purpose of producing more Whiting males if they were predestined to lives of marital torment?*

And so C. B. Whiting scrutinized Francine Robideaux, trying to envision some future day when he might want to beat her to death with a shovel. Thankfully, he was unable to call such a scene into vivid imaginative life. About the best he could do was contemplate the possibility that it had been unwise to go to war with God. If He could deliver unto you an unwanted moose, what was to prevent Him from delivering something even worse. Say, for instance, an unwanted woman. This would have been a worrisome contemplation had he not wanted this woman. But he did *want her. He was almost sure of it.*

His bride-to-be had other thoughts. "That would be a fine place for a gazebo, Charlie," she observed, indicating with her thin index finger a spot halfway down the bank. When Charles Beaumont Whiting did not immediately respond, Francine Robideaux repeated her observation, and this time her future husband thought he detected a slight edge to her tone. "Did you hear what I said, Charlie?"

He had. In truth, though he had no objection to gazebos in general, he was not entirely taken with the idea of erecting one as an architectural companion to a hacienda. This aesthetic reservation was not, however, the cause of his hesitation. No, the reason he hadn't responded was that no one had ever called him Charlie. From boyhood he had always been Charles, and his mother in particular had been adamant that the fine name she'd given him was not to be corrupted with more common nicknames, like Charlie or, even worse, Chuck. For a brief time, in college, his friends had called him Beaumont, and in Mexico he'd been Beau. More recently, his business acquaintances mostly referred to him as C.B., but they did so reverentially and would never have presumed to address him as Charlie.

Clearly, the time to set the record straight was now, but as he considered how best to suggest his preference for Charles over Charlie, he became aware that "now" had already passed into "then." Strange. Had anyone else called him Charlie, he'd have corrected that person before his or her voice had a chance to fall, but for some reason, with this woman whom he had asked on bended knee to be his bride, he'd delayed. A beat passed, and then another and another, until Charles Beaumont Whiting realized that he was mute with a new emotion. At first he noted only its unpleasant sensation, but eventually he identified it. The emotion was fear.

"I said . . ." his wife-to-be began a third time.

"*Yes, dear. An excellent idea,*" Charles Beaumont Whiting agreed and in that fateful moment became Charlie Whiting. *Later in life, he was fond of remarking, rather ruefully, that he always had the last word in all differences of opinion with his wife, and that—two words, actually—was, "Yes, dear." Had he known how many times he would repeat that phrase to this woman, how it would become the mantra of their marriage, he might well have recollected the river's invitation and committed himself to its current then and there and followed the moose downstream, thereby saving himself a great deal of misery and the price of the handgun he would purchase thirty years later for the purpose of ending his life.*

"*And would you mind putting out that awful cigar?*" Francine Robideaux added.

PART ONE

THE EMPIRE GRILL was long and low-slung, with windows
that ran its entire length, and since the building next door, a
Rexall drugstore, had been condemned and razed, it was now
possible to sit at the lunch counter and see straight down Empire
Avenue all the way to the old textile mill and its adjacent shirt factory.
Both had been abandoned now for the better part of two decades,
though their dark, looming shapes at the foot of the avenue's gentle
incline continued to draw the eye. Of course, nothing prevented a person from looking up Empire Avenue in the other direction, but Miles
Roby, the proprietor of the restaurant—and its eventual owner, he
hoped—had long noted that his customers rarely did.

No, their natural preference was to gaze down to where the street
both literally and figuratively dead-ended at the mill and factory, the
undeniable physical embodiment of the town's past, and it was the
magnetic quality of the old, abandoned structures that steeled Miles's
resolve to sell the Empire Grill for what little it would bring, just as
soon as the restaurant was his.

Just beyond the factory and mill ran the river that long ago had
powered them, and Miles often wondered if these old buildings were
razed, would the town that had grown up around them be forced to
imagine a future? Perhaps not. Nothing but a chain-link fence had
gone up in place of the Rexall, which meant, Miles supposed, that
diverting one's attention from the past was not the same as envisioning
and embarking upon a future. On the other hand, if the past were
razed, the slate wiped clean, maybe fewer people would confuse it with
the future, and that at least would be something. For as long as the

mill and factory remained, Miles feared, many would continue to believe against all reason that a buyer might be found for one or both, and that consequently Empire Falls would be restored to its old economic viability.

What drew Miles Roby's anxious eye down Empire this particular afternoon in early September was not the dark, high-windowed shirt factory where his mother had spent most of her adult working life or, just beyond it, the larger, brooding presence of the textile mill, but rather his hope that he'd catch a glimpse of his daughter, Tick, when she rounded the corner and began her slow, solitary trek up the avenue. Like most of her high school friends, Tick, a rail-thin sophomore, lugged all her books in a canvas L.L. Bean backpack and had to lean forward, as if into a strong headwind, to balance a weight nearly as great as her own. Oddly, most of the conventions Miles remembered from high school had been subverted. He and his friends had carried their textbooks balanced on their hips, listing first to the left, then shifting the load and listing to the right. They brought home only the books they would need that night, or the ones they *remembered* needing, leaving the rest crammed in their lockers. Kids today stuffed the entire contents of their lockers into their seam-stretched backpacks and brought it all home, probably, Miles figured, so they wouldn't have to think through what they'd need and what they could do without, thereby avoiding the kinds of decisions that might trail consequences. Except that this itself had consequences. A visit to the doctor last spring had revealed the beginnings of scoliosis, a slight curvature of Tick's spine, which worried Miles at several levels. "She's just carrying too much weight," the doctor explained, unaware, as far as Miles could tell, of the metaphorical implications of her remark. It had taken Tick most of the summer to regain her normal posture, and yesterday, after one day back at school, she was already hunched over again.

Instead of catching sight of his daughter, the one person in the world he wanted at that moment to see rounding the corner, Miles was instead treated to the sight of Walt Comeau, the person he least wanted to see—the one he could live happily without ever laying eyes on again—pulling into a vacant parking space in front of the Empire Grill. Walt's van was a rolling advertisement for its driver, who'd had THE SILVER FOX stenciled across the hood, just above the grill, and its vanity plates read FOXY I. The van was tall and Walt short, which meant he had to hop down from the running board, and something about the man's youthful bounce made Miles, who'd seen this both in real life and in his dreams just about every day for the past year, want to grab an ax handle, meet the Silver Fox at the door and stave his head in right there in the entryway.

Instead he turned back to the grill and flipped Horace Weymouth's burger, wondering if he'd already left it on too long. Horace liked his burgers bloody.

"So." Horace closed and folded his *Boston Globe* in anticipation of being fed, his inner clock apparently confirming that Miles had indeed waited too long. "You been out to see Mrs. Whiting yet?"

"Not yet," Miles said. He set up Horace's platter with tomato, lettuce, a slice of Bermuda onion and a pickle, plus the open-faced bun, then pressed down on the burger with his spatula, making it sizzle before slipping it onto the bun. "I usually wait to be summoned."

"I wouldn't," Horace counseled. "Somebody's got to inherit Empire Falls. It might as well be Miles Roby."

"I'd have a better chance of winning the MegaBucks lottery," Miles said, sliding the platter onto the counter and noticing, which he hadn't for a long time, the purple fibroid cyst that grew out of Horace's forehead. Had it gotten larger, or was it just that Miles had been away and was seeing it afresh after even a short absence? The cyst had taken over half of Horace's right eyebrow, where hairless skin stretched tight and shiny over the knot, its web of veins fanning outward from its dark center. One of the good things about small towns, Miles's mother had always maintained, was that they accommodated just about everyone; the lame and the disfigured were all your neighbors, and seeing them every day meant that after a while you stopped noticing what made them different.

Miles hadn't seen much in the way of physical oddity on Martha's Vineyard, where he and his daughter had vacationed last week. Almost everyone on the island appeared to be rich, slender and beautiful. When he'd remarked on this, his old friend Peter said that he should come live in L.A. for a while. There, he argued, ugliness was rapidly and systematically being bred out of the species. "He doesn't really mean L.A.," Peter's wife, Dawn, had corrected when Miles appeared dubious. "He means Beverly Hills." "And Bel Air," Peter added. "And Malibu," Dawn said. And then they named a baker's dozen other places where unattractiveness had been eradicated. Peter and Dawn were full of such worldly wisdom, which, for the most part, Miles enjoyed. The three had been undergraduates together at a small Catholic college outside of Portland, and he admired that they were barely recognizable as the students he'd known. Peter and Dawn had become other people entirely, and Miles concluded that this was what was supposed to happen, though it hadn't happened to him. If disappointed by their old friend's lack of personal evolution, they concealed that disappointment well, even going so far as to claim that he restored their faith in humanity by remaining the same old Miles. Since they apparently meant this as a compliment, Miles tried hard to take it that way. They did seem genuinely glad to see him every August, and even though each year he half expected his old friends not to renew the invitation for the following summer, he was always wrong.

Horace picked the thin slice of Bermuda off the plate with his thumb and forefinger, as if to suggest great offense at the idea that onions should be in such close proximity to anything he was expected to eat. "I don't eat onions, Miles. I know you've been away, but I haven't changed. I read the *Globe*, I write for the *Empire Gazette*, I never send Christmas cards, and I don't eat onions."

Miles accepted the onion slice and deposited it in the garbage. It was true he'd been slightly off all day, still sluggish and stupid from vacation, forgetting things that were second nature. He'd intended to work himself back in gradually by supervising the first couple shifts, but Buster, with whom Miles alternated at the grill, always took his revenge by going on a bender as soon as Miles returned from the island, forcing him back behind the grill before he was ready.

"She's better than MegaBucks," Horace said, still on the subject of Mrs. Whiting, who each year spent less and less time in Maine, wintering in Florida and doing what Miles's long dead Irish maternal grandmother, who liked to stay put, would have called "gallivanting." Apparently Mrs. Whiting had just returned from an Alaskan cruise. "If I was a member of the family I'd be out there kissing her bony ass every day."

Miles watched Horace assemble his burger, relieved to see a red stain spreading over the bun.

Miles Roby was not, of course, a member of Mrs. Whiting's family. What Horace referred to was the fact that the old woman's maiden name had been Robideaux, and some maintained that the Robys and the Robideauxs of Dexter County were, if you went back far enough, the same family. Miles's own father, Max, believed this to be true, though for him it was purely a matter of wishful thinking. Lacking any evidence that he and the richest woman in central Maine weren't related, Max decided they must be. Miles knew that if his father had been the one with the money and somebody named Robideaux felt entitled to even a dime of it, he naturally would've seen the whole thing differently.

Of course, it was a moot point. Mrs. Whiting had married all that money in the person of C. B. Whiting, who had owned the paper mill and the shirt factory and the textile mill before selling them all to multinational corporations so they could be pillaged and then closed. The Whiting family still owned half the real estate in Empire Falls, including the grill, which Miles had managed for Mrs. Whiting these last fifteen years with the understanding that the business would devolve upon him at her passing, an event Miles continued to anticipate without, somehow, being able to imagine it. What would happen to the rest of the old woman's estate was a matter of great speculation. Normally, it would have been inherited by her daughter, but Cindy Whiting had been in and out of the state mental hospital in Augusta all her adult life, and it was widely believed that Mrs. Whiting would never entrust her daughter with anything more than her continued maintenance required. In truth, no one in Dexter County knew much about Mrs. Whiting's actual wealth or her plans for it. She never dealt with local lawyers or accountants, preferring to employ a Boston firm that the Whitings had used for nearly a century. She did little to discourage the notion that a significant legacy would one day go to the town itself, but neither did she offer any concrete assurances. Mrs. Whiting was not known for philanthropy. In times of crisis, such as the most recent flood of the Knox River, she occasionally contributed, though she always insisted that the community match her donation. Similar restrictions were applied to seed money for a new wing of the hospital and a grant to upgrade computers at the high school. Such gifts, though sizable, were judged to be little more than shavings off the tip of a financial iceberg. When the woman was dead, it was hoped, the money would flow more freely.

Miles wasn't so sure. Mrs. Whiting's generosity toward the town, like that she extended to him, was puzzlingly ambiguous. Some years ago, for instance, she'd donated the decaying old Whiting mansion, which occupied a large section of the downtown, with the proviso that it be preserved. It was only after accepting her gift that the mayor and town council came to understand the extent of the burden they'd been handed. They could no longer collect taxes on the property, which they were not permitted to use for social events, and maintenance costs were considerable. Similarly, if Mrs. Whiting did end up giving the restaurant to Miles, he feared that the gift would be too costly to accept.

In fact, now that the mills were all closed down, it sometimes appeared that Mrs. Whiting had cornered the market on business failure. She owned most of the commercial space in town and was all too happy to help new enterprises start up in one of her buildings. But then rents had a way of going up, and none of the businesses seemed to get anywhere, nor did their owners when they appealed to Mrs. Whiting for more favorable terms.

"I don't know, Miles," Horace said. "You seem to have a special place in that old woman's heart. Her treatment of you is unique in my experience. The fact that she hasn't closed the grill down suggests just how deep her affection runs. Either that or she enjoys watching you suffer."

Though Miles understood this last observation to be a joke, he found himself—and not for the first time—considering whether it might not be the simple literal truth. Viewed objectively, Mrs. Whiting did appear to cut him more slack than was her custom, and yet there were times when Miles got the distinct impression that she bore him no particular fondness. Which probably explained why he was not all that eager to meet with her now, though he knew their annual meeting could not be postponed for long. Each autumn she left for Florida earlier than the last, and while their annual "State of the Grill" meetings were little more than a pro forma ritual, Mrs. Whiting refused to forgo them; and in her company he could not shake the feeling that for all these years the old woman had been expecting him to show her some sign—of what, he had no idea. Still, he left every encounter with the sense that he'd yet again failed some secret test.

THE BELL JINGLED above the door, and Walt Comeau danced inside, his arms extended like an old-fashioned crooner's, his silver hair slicked back on the sides, fifties style. "Don't let the stars get in your eyes," he warbled, "don't let the moon break your heart."

Several of the regulars at the lunch counter, knowing what was expected of them, swiveled on their stools, leaned into the aisle, right arms extended in a row, and returned, in a different key altogether, "Pa pa pa paya."

"Perry Como," Horace said when he realized, without actually looking, that the seat next to him at the counter had been filled. "Right on time."

"Big Boy," Walt said, addressing Miles, "you hear the news?"

"Oh, please," said Miles, who'd been hearing little else all morning. Over the weekend a black Lincoln Town Car with Massachusetts plates had been reported in the lot outside the textile mill. Last year it had been a BMW, the year before that a Cadillac limo. The color of the vehicle seemed to alternate between black and white, but the plates were always Massachusetts, which made Miles smile. The hordes of visitors who poured into Maine every summer were commonly referred to as Massholes, and yet when Empire Falls fantasized about deliverance, it invariably had Massachusetts plates.

"What?" Walt said, indignant. "You weren't even here."

"Let him tell you about it," Horace advised. "Then it'll be over."

Walt Comeau looked back and forth between Miles and Horace as if to determine who was the bigger fool, settling finally on Horace, probably because he'd spoken last. "All right, you explain it. Three guys in eight-hundred-dollar suits drive all the way up here from Boston on a Sunday morning, park outside the mill, hike down to the head of the falls in their black patent leather shoes, then stand there for half an hour pointing up at the mill. You tell me who they are and what they're doing."

Horace set his hamburger down and wiped his mouth with his napkin. "Hey, it's clear to me. They came to invest millions. For a while they were thinking about tech stocks, but then they thought, Hell, no. Let's go into textiles. That's where the *real* profits are. Then you know what they did? They decided not to build the factory in Mexico or Thailand where people work for about ten bucks a week. Let's drive up to Empire Falls, Maine, they said, and look at that gutted old shell of a factory that the river damn near washed away last spring and buy all new equipment and create hundreds of jobs, nothing under twenty dollars an hour."

Miles couldn't help smiling. Minus the sarcasm, this was pretty much the scenario he'd been listening to all morning. The annual sighting was born, as far as Miles could tell, of the same need that caused people to spot Elvis in the local Denny's. But why always autumn? Miles wondered. It seemed an odd season to spawn such desperate optimism. Maybe it had something to do with the kids all going back to school, giving their parents the leisure to contemplate the approach of another savage, relentless winter and to conjure up a pipe dream to help them through it.

"Hey," Walt said, sounding hurt. "All I'm saying is something nice *could* happen here someday. You never know. That's all I'm saying, okay?"

Horace had gone back to his hamburger, and this time he didn't bother to put it down or wipe his mouth before speaking. "Something nice," he repeated. "Is that what you think? That having money makes people nice?"

"Ah, to hell with you," Walt said, dismissing both men with a single wave of his hand. "Here's what I'd like to know, though, smart-ass. How can you sit here and eat one greasy hamburger after another, day after goddamn day? Don't you have any idea how bad that junk is for you?"

Horace, who had one bite of burger left, put it on his plate and looked up. "What I don't know is why you have to ruin my lunch every day. Why can't you leave people in peace?"

"Because I care about you," Walt said. "I can't help it."

"I wish you could," Horace said, pushing his platter away.

"Well, I can't." Walt pushed Horace's platter even farther down the counter and took a worn deck of cards out of his pocket, slapping it down in front of Horace. "I can't let you die before I figure out how you're beating me at gin."

Horace polished some hamburger grease into the countertop with his napkin before cutting the deck. "You should live so long. Hell, *I* should live so long," he said, watching the deal, content to wait until he had his whole hand before picking up any cards. He always gave the impression of having played all these hands before, as if the chief difficulty presented by each one was the boredom inherent in pretending over and over again that you didn't know how everything would eventually play out. By contrast, when Horace dealt, Walt picked up each card on the fly, identifying it eagerly, each hand promising an entirely new experience.

"Nope," he now said, arranging the cards in his hand one way, then another, uncertain as to which organizing principle—suits or numbers—would be more likely to guarantee victory. "I'm your best friend, Horace. You just don't know it. And I'll tell you something else you don't know. You don't know who your worst enemy is, either."

Horace, who seldom seemed to move more than a card or two before his hand made sense, rolled his eyes at Miles. "Who might that looking, that the seat next to him at the counter had been filled. "Right on time."

"Big Boy," Walt said, addressing Miles, "you hear the news?"

"Oh, please," said Miles, who'd been hearing little else all morning. Over the weekend a black Lincoln Town Car with Massachusetts plates had been reported in the lot outside the textile mill. Last year it had been a BMW, the year before that a Cadillac limo. The color of the vehicle seemed to alternate between black and white, but the plates were always Massachusetts, which made Miles smile. The hordes of visitors who poured into Maine every summer were commonly referred to as Massholes, and yet when Empire Falls fantasized about deliverance, it invariably had Massachusetts plates.

"What?" Walt said, indignant. "You weren't even here."

"Let him tell you about it," Horace advised. "Then it'll be over."

Walt Comeau looked back and forth between Miles and Horace as if to determine who was the bigger fool, settling finally on Horace, probably because he'd spoken last. "All right, you explain it. Three guys in eight-hundred-dollar suits drive all the way up here from Boston on a Sunday morning, park outside the mill, hike down to the head of the falls in their black patent leather shoes, then stand there for half an hour pointing up at the mill. You tell me who they are and what they're doing."

Horace set his hamburger down and wiped his mouth with his napkin. "Hey, it's clear to me. They came to invest millions. For a while they were thinking about tech stocks, but then they thought, Hell, no. Let's go into textiles. That's where the *real* profits are. Then you know what they did? They decided not to build the factory in Mexico or Thailand where people work for about ten bucks a week. Let's drive up to Empire Falls, Maine, they said, and look at that gutted old shell of a factory that the river damn near washed away last spring and buy all new equipment and create hundreds of jobs, nothing under twenty dollars an hour."

Miles couldn't help smiling. Minus the sarcasm, this was pretty much the scenario he'd been listening to all morning. The annual sighting was born, as far as Miles could tell, of the same need that caused people to spot Elvis in the local Denny's. But why always autumn? Miles wondered. It seemed an odd season to spawn such desperate optimism. Maybe it had something to do with the kids all going back to school, giving their parents the leisure to contemplate the approach of another savage, relentless winter and to conjure up a pipe dream to help them through it.

"Hey," Walt said, sounding hurt. "All I'm saying is something nice *could* happen here someday. You never know. That's all I'm saying, okay?"

Horace had gone back to his hamburger, and this time he didn't bother to put it down or wipe his mouth before speaking. "Something nice," he repeated. "Is that what you think? That having money makes people nice?"

"Ah, to hell with you," Walt said, dismissing both men with a single wave of his hand. "Here's what I'd like to know, though, smart-ass. How can you sit here and eat one greasy hamburger after another, day after goddamn day? Don't you have any idea how bad that junk is for you?"

Horace, who had one bite of burger left, put it on his plate and looked up. "What I don't know is why you have to ruin my lunch every day. Why can't you leave people in peace?"

"Because I care about you," Walt said. "I can't help it."

"I wish you could," Horace said, pushing his platter away.

"Well, I can't." Walt pushed Horace's platter even farther down the counter and took a worn deck of cards out of his pocket, slapping it down in front of Horace. "I can't let you die before I figure out how you're beating me at gin."

Horace polished some hamburger grease into the countertop with his napkin before cutting the deck. "You should live so long. Hell, *I* should live so long," he said, watching the deal, content to wait until he had his whole hand before picking up any cards. He always gave the impression of having played all these hands before, as if the chief difficulty presented by each one was the boredom inherent in pretending over and over again that you didn't know how everything would eventually play out. By contrast, when Horace dealt, Walt picked up each card on the fly, identifying it eagerly, each hand promising an entirely new experience.

"Nope," he now said, arranging the cards in his hand one way, then another, uncertain as to which organizing principle—suits or numbers—would be more likely to guarantee victory. "I'm your best friend, Horace. You just don't know it. And I'll tell you something else you don't know. You don't know who your worst enemy is, either."

Horace, who seldom seemed to move more than a card or two before his hand made sense, rolled his eyes at Miles. "Who might that be, Perry?" Horace asked, the way a man will when he already knows what's coming. It wasn't just these gin hands he'd played before.

Walt nodded at Miles. "It's Big Boy here," he said, to no one's surprise. "You keep eating his greasy burgers, you're going to look just like him, too, if you don't have a coronary first."

"You want some coffee, Walt?" Miles asked. "I always feel better about you undermining my business after I've coaxed eighty-five cents out of you."

"You *need* more customers like me," Walt replied, tossing a twenty on the counter. Among the many things Miles held against the Silver Fox was his compulsion to break large bills at every opportunity; even if his wallet was full of singles, he always paid for his coffee with a twenty or a fifty. Occasionally, he'd try to get Miles to break a hundred, enjoying the sport of Miles's refusal. "A cup of coffee costs you . . . what? A dime? Fifteen cents? And you get almost a buck for it, right? That's eighty-five cents profit. Not too shabby."

Miles poured each man a cup, then took Walt's twenty to the register. There was no point calling the Silver Fox on the intentional vagaries of his arithmetic. "After I refill it four or five times, how much have I made then?"

When the bell over the door jingled again, Miles glanced up and saw his younger brother enter, a newspaper tucked under his ruined arm. Noting where Walt Comeau was seated, he located a stool at the other end of the counter. When Miles poured him a cup of coffee, David, who had already unfolded the front section and begun reading, met his eye and glanced down the counter at Walt Comeau before returning to his paper. For the most part the brothers understood each other perfectly, especially their silences. This one suggested that in David's view Miles had not returned from his vacation any smarter than he was before he left.

"You're pretty well prepped," Miles said, referring to the private party David was catering that evening. "I brought you back a couple jars of that lobster paste for bisque."

David nodded, pouring milk into his coffee with his good hand. "Tell me something," he said. "Why do you allow him in here?"

"It's against the law to refuse service."

"So's murder," David said, picking up the newspaper again. "It'd be an elegant solution, just the same."

Miles tried to imagine it. Assuming he could get ahold of a handgun, what kind of man, he wondered, would walk up to another human being—even Walt Comeau—and squeeze another death into the world? Not Miles Roby, concluded Miles Roby.

"Hey," his brother said when Miles started back down the counter, "thanks for the paste. How was the Vineyard?"

"I think Peter and Dawn might be calling it quits," Miles told him.

David didn't look very surprised, or interested, for that matter. The idea of old college friends seemed to bore him, perhaps because David himself had never gone beyond high school, except for a single semester at the Maine Culinary Institute.

"I could be wrong," Miles continued. He hated the idea of Peter and Dawn divorcing, which, if true, would take some getting used to. In fact, he still wasn't used to the idea of his own divorce. "It was just an impression."

"You didn't answer my question," David observed, without looking up from the paper.

Miles tried to remember. Had there been a question? More than one?

"How . . . was . . . the Vineyard?"

"Oh, right," Miles said, aware that this was precisely the sort of thing his soon-to-be ex-wife always complained of: that he never really listened to her. For twenty years he'd tried to convince Janine that this wasn't the case, or at least wasn't precisely the case. It wasn't that he didn't hear her questions and requests. It was more that they always provoked a response she hadn't anticipated. "I'm not ignoring you," he insisted, to which she invariably replied, "You might as well be."

"Well?" his brother wanted to know. About the Vineyard.

"Just the same," Miles told him. Of all the places in the world he couldn't hope to afford, the Vineyard was his favorite.

"YOU KNOW WHAT you need in here, Big Boy?" Walt called from down at his end of the counter. Every time he lost another hand of gin to Horace, he thought of some further improvement for the Empire Grill.

"What's that, Walt?" Miles sighed, filling salt shakers at midcounter.

"You need to stop with this swill and start serving Green Mountain Coffee." In his own opinion Walt was on the cutting edge of all that was new and good in the world. In his fitness club, which he was forever hounding Miles to join, promising washboard abs, he'd recently introduced protein shakes, and he thought these might prove to be a hot item at the grill as well. Miles, of course, had ignored all such suggestions, thereby reinforcing Walt's contention that he was a congenitally backward man, destined to run a backward establishment. Walt expressed this view pretty much every day, leaving unanswered only the question of why he himself, a forward man in every sense of the word, chose to spend so much time in this backward venue.

"I bet you couldn't pass a blind taste test," said Horace, who usually took Miles's part in these disputes, especially since Miles appeared reluctant to defend himself against the relentless assaults on his personal philosophy.

"You kidding? Green Mountain Coffee? Night-and-day difference," Walt said.

When the bell above the door tinkled again, Miles looked up and saw that this time it was his daughter, which meant that unless someone had given her a ride, she'd walked all the way up Empire Avenue from the river without his noticing. For some reason, this possibility unnerved him. Since he and Janine had separated, a separation of a different sort had occurred between himself and Tick, the exact nature of which he'd been trying for a long time to put his finger on. He wouldn't have blamed his daughter if she'd felt betrayed by his agreeing to divorce her mother, but apparently she didn't. She'd understood from the start that it was Janine's idea, and as a result she'd been much tougher on her mother than on Miles, so tough that simple fairness had required him to remind her that the person who wants out of a marriage isn't necessarily the cause of its failure. He suspected, however, that whatever had changed in their relationship had more to do with himself than with his daughter. Since spring he couldn't seem to get Tick to stand still long enough to get a good fix on her. She was maturing, of course, becoming a young woman instead of a kid, and he grasped that there were certain things going on with her that he didn't understand because he wasn't supposed to. Still, it troubled him to feel so out of sync. Too often he found himself needing to see her, as if only her physical presence could reassure him of her well-being; yet when she did appear, she seemed different from the girl he'd been needing and worrying about. The week they'd spent together on the Vineyard had been wonderful, and by the end of it he'd felt much more in tune with Tick than at any time since he and Janine had separated. But since they'd come home, the disconnected feeling had returned with a vengeance, as if losing sight of her might lead to tragic consequences. Even now, instead of relief he was visited by an alternative scenario—the screech of tires somewhere down the block, Tick's inert body lying in the street, an automobile speeding away, dragging her enormous backpack. Which had *not* happened, he reminded himself, quickly swallowing his panic.

As she did every afternoon, Tick gave Walt Comeau wide berth, pretending not to see the arm he stretched out to her. "Hi, Uncle David," she said, rounding the far end of the counter and giving him a peck on the cheek.

"Hello, Beautiful," David said, helping her off with her backpack, which thudded to the floor of the restaurant hard enough to make the water glasses and salt and pepper shakers jump along the lunch counter. "You gonna be my helper today?"

"Whatcha got in that pack, Sweetie Pie? Rocks?" Walt Comeau called the length of the counter.

Rather than acknowledge his existence, Tick went over to Miles and buried her face in his apron, stretching her arms around his waist and hooking her fingers at his back. "I've got Abba in my head," she told him. "Make them go away."

"Sorry," Miles told her, drawing his child to him, feeling the smile spread across his face at her nearness, at her confidence in his ability to dispel the bad magic of old pop groups. Not that she was a child anymore, not really. "Did you hear them on the radio?"

"No," she admitted. "They're *his* fault." Meaning Walt. And with this accusation she pulled away from her father and grabbed an apron.

The reason it was Walt Comeau's fault was that Janine, Tick's mother, played "Mama Mia" and "Dancing Queen" in her beginning and intermediate aerobics classes at Walt's fitness club, then hummed these same songs at home. Only her advanced steppers were deemed ready for the rigors of Barry Manilow and the Copa Cabana.

"Your dad says you had a good time on the Vineyard?" David said when Tick passed by on her way to the kitchen with a tub of dirty dishes.

"I want to live there," she confessed, like someone who saw no harm in confessing a sin she was never likely to have the opportunity to commit. "There's a bookstore for sale on the beach road, but Daddy won't buy it." The door swung shut behind her.

"How much?" David wondered, tossing down his paper, grabbing a clean apron and joining his brother at mid-counter. He still had partial use of his damaged hand, but not much strength and very little dexterity. "Save me half an hour and tie this, will you?"

Miles had already set down the salt shakers he was filling.

"So?" David said when the knot cinched.

"So what?"

"How much was the bookstore? God! How come you can recite twenty-five consecutive breakfast orders and not remember a simple question I asked you two seconds ago?"

"More like a book barn, actually," Miles said, since that was what it had once been. There'd been enough room downstairs to sell new books and set up a small café, since people seemed to think those belonged in bookstores now. The upstairs could be cleaned up and devoted to used books. There was even a small cottage on the property. The same couple had owned and run the business for about twenty years but now the wife was sick, and her husband was trying to talk himself into letting it go. Their kids didn't want any part of it after going away to college.

"How come you know all that and not the price?" David wondered when Miles finished explaining.

"I didn't actually see the listing. Peter just pointed the place out. I don't think he knew the asking price. He isn't interested in running a bookstore."

"They got a fitness club over there, Big Boy?" Walt wanted to know.

"I don't know, Walt," Miles told him, trying to sound neutral about the idea. If anything in the world could ruin the island for him, it would be Walt Comeau's presence. Of course, the idea of a blowhard like the Silver Fox anywhere outside of Empire Falls was absurd, but Miles didn't dare laugh. A year ago Walt had joked that if Miles wasn't careful he was going to steal his wife, and then he'd gone ahead and done it.

Walt scratched his chin thoughtfully, while contemplating a discard. "I figure my club here's doing pretty well. Practically runs itself. Now might be a good time to expand." He sounded as if his only obstacle was the matter of timing. The Silver Fox liked to imply that money was never a consideration, that every bank in Dexter County was eager to loan him whatever capital he didn't have. Miles doubted this was true, but it might be. He'd also doubted that his soon-to-be-ex-wife was the sort of woman to be taken in by Walt Comeau's bravado, and he'd certainly been wrong about that.

"Go ahead and split if you want," David told him. "He'll be wanting to arm-wrestle you in a minute."

Miles shrugged. "I think he just comes in to let me know there's no hard feelings."

This elicited a chuckle. "About the way he stole your wife?"

"Some sins trail their own penance," Miles said softly, after glancing toward the back room, where Tick could be heard loading dirty dishes into the ancient Hobart. One of the few things Miles and Janine had been able to agree on when their marriage came apart was that they wouldn't speak ill of each other in front of their daughter. The agreement, Miles knew, worked much to his advantage, since most of the time he had no desire to speak ill of his ex-wife, whereas Janine always appeared to be strangling on her wretched opinion of him. Of course, all the other agreements they'd arrived at—such as letting her stay in the house until it sold and the one that gave her the better car and most of their possessions—worked pretty much in Janine's favor, which left Miles staggering with debt.

"Tick really had a good time?"

Miles nodded. "You should've seen her. She was like her old self, before all the shit started raining down on her. She smiled for a solid week."

"Good."

"She met a boy, too."

"That always helps."

"Don't tease her about it, now."

"Okay," David promised, though it was one that would be hard for him to keep.

Miles took off his apron and tossed it in the hamper by the door. "You should take a week yourself. Go someplace."

His brother shrugged. "Why invite disaster? I'm down to one arm as it is. I ever let myself go someplace fun, I might start misbehaving, and then I'd have to flip your burgers with my toes."

He was right, of course. Miles knew his brother had been sober since the afternoon three years ago when, returning from a hunting trip up in The County, David, drunk, had fallen asleep at the wheel and run his pickup off a mountain road into a ravine. Airborne, the truck had hit a tree and there parted company with its unseatbelted driver, the vehicle careening a good hundred yards down the ravine and coming to rest well out of sight in the thick woods. David, thrown free of the cab, had gotten snagged by his hunting vest in the upper branches of a tree and hung there, some fifty feet above the ground, drifting in and out of consciousness, his arm shattered in several places and four ribs fractured, until he was discovered half frozen the next morning by a group of hunters, one of whom had stationed himself beneath the very tree David improbably dangled from, unable to utter a sound. If his bladder hadn't given way, as David was fond of remarking, he'd still be twisting there in the frigid wind, a sack of tough L.L. Bean outerwear full of bleached bones.

That lonely, hallucinatory night had proved more effective than all the therapies he'd undergone in the various substance abuse clinics he'd been admitted to over the previous decade. His old Empire Falls drinking buddies, most of whom were still roaring around Dexter County in beer-laden snowmobiles, occasionally sought David out, hoping to nudge him gently off the wagon by reminding him how much more fun the drinking life was, but so far he'd resisted their invitations. The year before, he'd bought a small camp in the woods off Small Pond Road, and he said that whenever he felt the urge to stare at the world through the brown glass of an empty beer bottle, all he had to do was walk outside on his deck and look up into the pines and listen again to the horrible sound the wind made in their upper branches. Miles hoped this was true. He'd been estranged from his brother at the time of the accident, and continued to observe David warily, not doubting his brother's intention to reform, just his ability. He still smoked a little dope, Miles knew, and probably even had a small marijuana patch out in the woods, like half his rural Maine neighbors, but he hadn't had a drink since the accident and he still wore the orange vest that had saved his life.

Miles surveyed the restaurant, trying to see what he'd left undone. One week away had been sufficient to make it all seem unfamiliar. He'd spent most of yesterday trying to remember where things went. Only when he got busy and didn't have time to think did his body remember where they were. Today had been better, though not much. "Okay," he said. "You think of anything you need?"

David grinned. "All kinds of stuff, but let's not get started."

"Okay," Miles agreed.

"You should think about it, Miles," David said from his knees, where he was checking stores under the counter.

"About what?"

His brother just looked up at him.

"What?" Miles repeated.

David shrugged, went back to searching under the counter.

"Number one, I can't afford it. At least not until I can sell this place. Number two, Janine'd never let me take Tick, and Tick is the one thing I won't let her have. And number three, who'd look after Dad?"

His brother stood, a mega-pack of napkins wedged under the elbow of his bad arm, a reminder that Miles had forgotten to fill the dispensers. "Number one, you don't know if you can afford it because you never found out how much it cost. The owner might be open to a little creative financing for the right buyer. Number two, you could win Tick in court if you were willing to go there and duke it out. You're not the one who has to worry about being found an unfit parent. And number three, Max Roby is the most self-sufficient man on the face of the earth. He only looks and acts helpless. So when you say you can't, what you really mean is that it wouldn't be easy, right?"

"Have it your way, David," said Miles, who didn't feel like arguing. "Give me those."

But when he reached for the napkins, his brother turned deftly away. "Go."

"David, give me the damn napkins," Miles said. It was an easy job for a man with two good hands, a hard one for somebody with only one, and it did not escape Miles's attention that this seemed to be his brother's point. It would be difficult, but he'd do it anyway. For a man who'd hung by his vest fifty feet up in a tree and nearly frozen to death as a result of his own stupidity, David had always been strangely impatient with the failings of others.

"Go on. Get out of here."

Miles shook his head in surrender. "Did he come in at all last week?"

"Max? Three afternoons, actually."

"You didn't let him near the register, I hope?" Their father could not be trusted around money, though Miles and David had argued for years about the boundaries of his dishonesty. In Miles's opinion, there weren't any. David thought there were, even if they were not always easy to locate. For instance, he believed Max would take money out of his sons' pockets, but not out of the restaurant's cash register.

"I did pay him under the table, though."

"I wish you wouldn't," Miles said.

"I know you do, but why not pay him the way he wants? What difference does it make?"

"For one thing it's against the law. For another, Mrs. Whiting would have a cow if she thought I was doing anything off the books."

"She'd probably prefer it, if she understood there'd be more money left over for her."

"Possibly. It might also start her wondering. If I play fast and loose with the government, maybe I'm playing fast and loose with her, too."

David nodded the way you do when you've been given an inadequate explanation and decide to accept it anyway. "Okay, I got another question for you," he said, looking directly at Miles. "What makes you think that woman is ever going to give you this restaurant?"

"She said she would."

David nodded again. "I don't know, Miles," he said.

ONLY ONE TUB of dirty lunch dishes remained, but it was a big one, so Miles lugged it into the kitchen and set it on the drainboard, stopping there to listen to the Hobart chug and whir, steam leaking from inside its stainless steel frame. They'd had this dishwasher for, what, twenty years? Twenty-five? He was pretty sure it was there when Roger Sperry first hired him back in high school. It couldn't possibly have much more life in it, and if Miles had to guess when it would give out, it'd probably be the day after the restaurant became his. He'd spoken to Mrs. Whiting about replacing it, but a Hobart was a big-ticket item and the old woman wouldn't hear of any such thing while it was still running. When Miles was feeling generous, he reminded himself that seventy-something-year-old women probably didn't enjoy being told that things were old and worn-out, that they'd already lived years beyond a normal life expectancy. In less charitable moods, he suspected his employer was shrewdly determined to time the obsolescence of every machine in the restaurant—the Hobart, the Garland range, the grill, the milk machine—to her own ultimate demise, thus minimizing her gift to him as much as possible.

Their arrangement, struck nearly twenty years ago now—another lifetime, it seemed to Miles—when Roger Sperry fell ill, was that he would run the restaurant for the remainder of Mrs. Whiting's life, then inherit the place. The deal had been struck in secret because Miles knew his mother would object to his dropping out of college in his senior year; for him to mortgage his future in order to be nearby during her illness would surely fill her with not just despair but also fury. Mrs.

Whiting herself had seemed aware that their fait accompli was necessary, that once Grace learned of the arrangement she would talk Miles out of this futile gesture and remind him that she was going to die regardless, that compromising his own prospects was so perverse as to render meaningless her sacrifices on his behalf. Miles knew all this too, and so he had conspired with Mrs. Whiting to give her no such opportunity.

His mother's illness aside, taking over the Empire Grill had not seemed like such a terrible idea at the time. As a history major, Miles was coming to understand that it was unlikely he'd be able to find a job without a graduate degree, and there was no money for that. He'd started working at the restaurant during his junior year of high school, returning summers and holidays after going away to college, so no aspect of the restaurant's operation was beyond him; and while the living it promised would be hard, its rewards meager by the world's reckoning, by local standards he would make out all right. Why *not* run the joint for a few years and save some money? He could always finish school later. Mrs. Whiting would just have to understand.

Of course, all that was before the textile mill closed and the population of Empire Falls began to dwindle as families moved away in search of employment. And Miles, being young, did not know, since there was no way he could, that he'd never love the restaurant as Roger Sperry had, or that the other man's affection for it had long been the primary engine of its survival. Despite his youth, Miles did understand that people didn't go to places like the Empire Grill for the food. After only two or three training shifts he was a far better short-order cook than his mentor. Roger proudly proclaimed him a natural, by which he probably meant that Miles remembered what customers asked him for and then gave it to them, something Roger himself seldom managed to do. If he intuited any of Miles's shortcomings, he was too fond of the boy to share them with him.

Only after taking over the restaurant did Miles begin to realize that his relationship to the patrons of the Empire Grill had changed profoundly. Before, he'd been the smart kid—Grace Roby's boy—who was going off to college to make something of himself, and thus had been the object of much gentle, good-natured ridicule. The men at the lunch counter were forever quizzing him about things—the operation of backhoes, say, or the best spot to sink a septic tank—they imagined he must be learning about at college. His complete lack of wisdom on these subjects led them to wonder out loud just what the hell they were teaching down there in Portland. Often they didn't speak to Miles directly, but through Roger Sperry, as though an interpreter already were necessary. After Roger's death, the food improved in inverse proportion to the conversation. The men at the lunch counter wouldn't have said as much to Miles, but in their opinion he spent too much time with his back to them, attending to their sputtering hamburgers rather than their stories and grievances and jokes. While appreciative of his competence, they began to suspect that he had little interest in their conversation and, moreover, was unhappy in general. Roger Sperry had always been so glad to see them that he botched their orders; half the fun of the Empire Grill had been razzing him for these failures. Under Miles's competent stewardship, the Empire Grill, never terribly profitable, had gone into a long, gentle decline almost imperceptible without the benefit of time-lapse photography, until one day it was suddenly clear that the diner was *un*profitable, and so it had remained for years.

Still, Miles often sensed regret in Mrs. Whiting's demeanor when she recalled her promise to bequeath him the restaurant. Sometimes she seemed to blame him for its decline and wondered out loud why she needed the aggravation of a business that produced so little revenue. But on other occasions—and there had been several of these—when Miles himself had become discouraged and offered the same argument to his employer, Mrs. Whiting quickly retreated and urged him not to give up, reminding him that the Empire Grill was a landmark, that it was the only non-fast-food establishment in town, and that Empire Falls, if its residents were to remain at all hopeful about the future, needed the grill to survive, even if it didn't thrive.

Even more mysterious was the feeling Miles had that Mrs. Whiting wasn't altogether pleased by recent signs that business was picking up. During the past nine months, thanks to a bold initiative by David, the restaurant was actually beginning to turn around, and for several months that spring had actually turned a small profit. When he expressed this optimistic view to Mrs. Whiting, expecting her to be pleased by the modest reversal of fortune, she regarded both the news and its bearer suspiciously, as if she either didn't believe the numbers with which she was being presented or feared that the Roby boys might be trying to put something over on her.

Miles knew Mrs. Whiting had put the bequest in her will, because she showed him the pertinent section of the document all those years ago. What he didn't know, of course, was whether, as David cautioned, she had ever amended it. That was possible, of course, but he continued to maintain, at least to his brother, that if Mrs. Whiting said she was going to leave him the restaurant, she'd do so. However, he had to admit it would be entirely in character for the old woman to ensure that the restaurant at the time of the transfer would be worth as little as possible. And in the meantime, it was his own responsibility to keep the Hobart running, with rubber bands, if necessary.

Tick was seated on the opposite drainboard, listlessly munching a granola bar, waiting for the machine to complete its cycle. "I had an Empire Moment on the way here," she said, without much enthusiasm. "Not a great one, though. The flower shop. Mixed B.O.K.A.Y."

This was a game they'd been playing for nearly a year, finding unintentional humor in the form of gaffes in the *Empire Gazette*, misspellings in advertisements for local stores, lapses in logic on printed signs like the one on the brick wall that surrounded the old empty shirt factory: NO TRESPASSING WITHOUT PERMISSION. They referred to the pleasure of these discoveries as "Empire Moments," and Tick was becoming disconcertingly adept at identifying them. Last month, down in Fairhaven, she'd noticed the sign outside the town's one shabby little rumored-to-be-gay bar whose entrance was being renovated: ENTER IN REAR. Miles was startled that his sixteen-year-old daughter had seen the humor in this, but he was proud too. Still, he wondered if Janine wasn't right. She'd disapproved of the game from the start, viewing it as yet another opportunity for the two of them to pretend superiority to everyone else, especially herself.

"Good eye," Miles nodded. "I'll look for it." By rule they always confirmed each other's sightings.

"I can do that," Tick said when she saw her father start scraping dishes into the garbage and stacking them in the plastic rack for the next load.

"Never doubted it," her father assured her. "How was school?"

She shrugged. "Okay."

There was precious little Miles would have changed about his daughter, but to his way of thinking far too many things in Tick's life were "okay." She was a smart kid, one who knew the difference between first-rate, mediocre and piss-poor, but like most kids her age she seemed bored by such distinctions. How was the movie? Okay. How were the french fries? Okay. How's your sprained ankle feeling? Okay. Everything was pretty much okay, even when it wasn't, even when in fact it was piss-poor. When the entire emotional spectrum, from despair to ecstasy, could be summed up by a single four-letter word, what was a parent to do? Even more troubling was his suspicion that "okay" was designed specifically as a conversation stopper, employed in hopes that the person who'd asked the question would simply go away.

The trick, Miles had learned, was not to go away. You didn't ask more probing questions, because they, too, would be met with this monosyllabic evasion. The trick was silence. If there was a trick.

"I made a new friend," Tick finally elaborated once the Hobart had shuddered to a halt and she'd raised the door to extract the tray of clean dishes.

Miles rinsed his hands and went over to where Tick was stacking the warm plates. He took one down from the shelf and checked it, relieved to find it squeaky clean. The Hobart would live.

"Candace Burke. She's in my art class. She stole an Exacto knife today."

"What for?"

Tick shrugged. "I guess she didn't have one. She starts all her sentences with oh-my-God-oh-my-God. Like, Oh-my-God-oh-my-God my mascara's running. Or, Oh-my-God-oh-my-God, you're even skinnier than last year."

This last, Miles suspected, was not a theoretical example. Tick, always stick-thin, was often accused of being anorexic. Last year she'd even been called into the nurse's office and questioned about her eating habits. In fact, Miles and Janine had been called in as well. This was before Janine herself lost so much weight, so she and Miles, sitting there in the school counselor's tiny office, did seem to suggest that Tick couldn't possibly have come by her reedlike body honestly.

Miles tried to think if he knew this Candace Burke. There were several Burke families in town. "What's she look like?"

"Fat."

"A lot or a little?"

"She's fat like I'm skinny."

"In other words, not very?" Miles ventured. In mid-adolescence his daughter was hard to compliment. The truth was that he thought her a heartbreakingly beautiful girl, and often tried to explain that it was her intelligence, her wit, that was keeping her from being more popular with boys. "Which Burke is she, I wonder?"

Tick shrugged. "She lives with her mother and her mother's new boyfriend down on Water Street. She says we've got a lot in common. I think she's in love with Zack. She keeps saying, 'Oh-my-God-oh-my-God, he's *so* good-looking. How can you *stand* it? I mean, like, he was yours, and now he's not.'"

"Did you tell her she's not missing much?" Even now, months after their breakup, the mere mention of Zack Minty, Tick's former boyfriend, was enough to make Miles grind his teeth. His fondest hope was that Donny, the boy Tick had met on the Vineyard, would free his daughter from any lingering attraction she might feel for a boy who, like his father and grandfather before him, bore more or less constant watching.

His daughter's pause did little to reassure him. "Here's the thing," she finally said. "Now that I'm not with Zack anymore, I don't have a single friend." Tick's two best friends had moved away in the last six months.

"Except Candace," Miles pointed out.

"Oh-my-God-oh-my-God!" she squealed in mock horror, "I forgot Candace!"

"And you forgot me," Miles pointed out.

Tick shrugged, serious now. "I know."

"And your uncle David."

A frown, a shrug, an apologetic "I know."

"And your mother."

Just a hint of a frown. When he didn't press further, she let him take her in his arms and surrendered limply to his awkward, overlarge embrace. Usually when Tick felt a bear hug coming, she'd position her body sideways, so one of her shoulders would dig under his breastbone. It was Janine who had explained what was going on, that their daughter's late-developing breasts were probably sore; her explanation made it clear that Janine herself hadn't cared all that much for his embraces. "I know we're not the kind of friends you had in mind," Miles told his daughter. "But we're not nobody."

A sniffle now, her nose buried deep in his chest. "I know."

"You going to write Donny?"

"What for? I'll never see him again."

Miles shrugged. "Who knows?"

"Me," she said, pulling away from him now. "And you."

He let her go back to unloading the Hobart. "You got homework?"

She shook her head.

"You want me to come back in a couple hours and run you home?"

"Mom said she'd come by," she said. "If she forgets, the idiot can do it."

"Hey," Miles said, and waited until she turned around and looked at him. "Go easy. He's trying. He just doesn't know how to . . . *be* around you."

"He could try being dead."

"Tick."

"Why can't you just go ahead and admit how much you hate him?"

Because he might not be able to stop there, was why. Because when David had suggested murder as a solution to the Silver Fox's daily visits, Miles had almost been able to imagine it.

"BIG BOY!" Walt Comeau bellowed when Miles emerged from the kitchen. "Come over here a minute."

Walt had taken his outer shirt off now, Miles noticed. He always wore white T-shirts with the logo of his fitness club over the left pectoral, and he always wore them a size too small, so everyone could admire his still-rippling-at-fifty torso and biceps. David had been right, of course. The Silver Fox was about to plant an elbow on the Formica counter and challenge Miles to arm-wrestle.

"Be right there," he called, then turned to David, who was handing napkins to Horace to stuff in the dispensers. "You got help tonight?"

"Charlene," David said. "I think she just pulled in."

"You want me to stop by later?"

"Nope."

Miles shrugged.

David grinned at him. "You're out the back, aren't you."

"You bet."

Behind the restaurant, the first slot, beside the Dumpster, was occupied by Miles's ten-year-old Jetta, the next one by Charlene's even more dilapidated Hyundai Excel. He tried to make enough noise in his approach so as not to startle her, but Charlene's radio was on loud enough that she jumped anyway when he appeared at her door.

"Jesus, Miles," she croaked in the clenched-toothed manner of pot smokers, once she'd rolled down the window. Sweet smoke escaped along with an old Rolling Stones song. "Give me a coronary, why don't you? I thought you were that asshole cop." Meaning Jimmy Minty.

"Sorry," Miles said, though in fact he wasn't entirely displeased. Most women saw Miles coming and said so. Janine clearly had. "Don't imagine you snuck up on me, Miles, because you didn't," she'd told him after accepting his proposal of marriage. That proposal had certainly taken *him* by surprise, and he'd taken this as an indication that Janine might be surprised too, but she wasn't. The World's Most Transparent Man, she called him. "Don't ever consider a life of crime," she advised. "You decide to rob a bank, the cops will know which one before you do."

"How did things go last week?" he asked Charlene.

"Slow," she said. "Dinners picked up, though."

"They've *been* picking up."

"Some of the college kids are filtering back in."

Dinners were a relatively new thing. Until a year ago the restaurant was open only for breakfast and lunch, but David had suggested opening for dinner on weekends and trying to attract a different clientele, an idea opposed by Mrs. Whiting, who feared that they'd lose their old tried-and-true customers. Miles had managed to convince her that, for the most part, tried-and-true was done and gone. In the end she'd grudgingly consented, but only after being reassured that they wouldn't ask for an advertising budget or make any changes in the breakfast and lunch menus or pester her for expensive redecoration to accompany the newer, more sophisticated dinner service.

At David's suggestion they began by inviting students who wrote restaurant reviews for the college paper to a free meal. The college was seven miles away, in Fairhaven, and even Miles hadn't believed that many students would make the trek, not when their parents were already shelling out more than twenty-five grand a year for tuition, room and board. But apparently there was money left over. When students started frequenting the Empire Grill, the cars parked out front— some of them, anyway—were BMWs and Audis. Summer had slowed some after this luxury fleet returned to Massachusetts and Connecticut, but Friday and Saturday nights still did well enough to justify staying open. David's other brainstorm was also working out: during the week the restaurant now catered private parties.

"You and David think you can handle tonight okay?"

"In our sleep. Rehearsal dinner for twenty people."

"Okay," Miles said, not quite able to conceal his disappointment at not being needed.

Charlene, seeming to understand all this, changed the subject. "You and Tick have a good vacation?"

"Great," he said. "I wish I hadn't been so enthusiastic, actually. Now Walt's thinking about opening a fitness club on the island."

"I saw his van out front," she said. "You want me to go in there and wither his dick?"

"Feel free," Miles said, knowing that it was well within her power. Charlene, at forty-five, was still more than enough woman to produce the same effect among the smug jocks from the college. "I'm out of here, anyway."

"You shouldn't let him run you off, Miles."

"I'm grateful he shows up. Wasn't for him, I'd probably never leave the premises." Since he and Janine separated, Miles had been living in the apartment above the restaurant. The plan had been to fix it up, make it livable, but after six months he still hadn't done much. Half the available living space was still occupied by cardboard boxes from the storage room in the basement, supplies that had been moved upstairs years before when the river flooded. Miles also suspected something was wrong with the apartment's heating system, since in cold weather he often woke up with headaches, feeling groggy and half asphyxiated. Last April he'd even considered asking Janine if he could sack out in the back bedroom for a while until the headaches went away, but when he went over to ask her, he discovered the Silver Fox had all but moved in. Better to asphyxiate above the Empire Grill, he'd decided.

"Well, if you're going somewhere, I wish you'd leave and let me finish this joint," Charlene told him.

"Go ahead and finish. Who's stopping you?"

"You. You know I don't feel comfortable smoking dope around you."

Since this was a vaguely insulting thing to say, Miles felt compelled to ask why.

"Because you're the kind of man who can never quite manage to conceal his disapproval."

Miles sighed, supposing this must be true. Janine had always said the same thing. Odd, though, the way other people saw you. Miles had always thought of himself as a model of tolerance.

CHAPTER 2

FATHER MARK, returning late in the afternoon from visiting his parish shut-ins, found Miles around back of St. Catherine's staring up at the steeple. As a boy Miles had been a climber, so fearless that he'd driven his mother into paroxysms of terror. When it was time for dinner, she'd come looking for him, always searching at ground level, which delighted him—he loved to call down to her from the air, forcing her to look up and locate him among the blue sky's tangled branches, her slender hand rushing to cover her mouth. At the time, he'd concluded she lacked the gift of memory, always expecting him on the ground when time after time he was in the air. Now a father himself, he knew how frightened she must've been. She hadn't looked up because there were too many trees, too many branches, too many dangers. Only when Miles swung safely down and landed at her feet was she able to smile, even as she scolded him into a promise she knew he would never keep. "You're a born climber," she'd admit on their way home. "What heights you'll scale when you're a man! I don't dare even think."

Now it was Miles who didn't dare even think. Of climbing, anyway. Somewhere along the line he'd become terrified of heights, and the idea of painting the steeple made him weak in the knees.

"When I was a little boy," Father Mark said, "I used to think God actually lived up there."

"In the steeple?" Miles said.

Father Mark nodded. "I thought when we sang hymns we were calling to Him to come down and be among us. Which of course we were. But the literal proximity was reassuring." The two men shook hands.

Miles had changed into his paint-spattered clothes but hadn't started in yet, so he was still dry. The sky, in the time since Miles left the grill, had grown ominous. "God Himself, a couple stories up . . . so close."

"I was just thinking how far *away* it is," Miles admitted. "But then I was contemplating painting it."

"That does makes a difference," Father Mark said.

"Actually I wasn't contemplating painting so much as falling."

Interesting, Miles thought. Like himself, Father Mark, as a child, had been reassured by the imagined proximity of God, whereas adults, perhaps because they so often were up to no good, took more comfort from His remoteness. Though Miles didn't think of himself as a man up to no good, he did prefer the notion of an all-loving God to that of an all-knowing one. It pleased him to imagine God as someone like his mother, someone beleaguered by too many responsibilities, too dog-tired to monitor an energetic boy every minute of the day, but who, out of love and fear for his safety, checked in on him whenever she could. Was this so crazy? Surely God must have other projects besides Man, just as parents had responsibilities other than raising their children? Miles liked the idea of a God who, when He at last had the opportunity to return His attention to His children, might shake His head with wonder and mutter, "Jesus. Look what they're up to now." A dis-tractible God, perhaps, one who'd be startled to discover so many of His children way up in trees since the last time He looked. A God whose hand would go rushing to His mouth in fear in that instant of recognition that—good God!—that kid's going to hurt himself. A God who could be surprised by unanticipated pride—glory be, that boy *is* a climber!

An idle, daydream deity, this, Miles had to admit. In truth, when God looked down upon His mischievous children, they were usually up to far worse than climbing trees.

If there were such a deity, though, and if He'd ever feared that Miles would hurt himself, He could quit worrying anytime now. For all his early promise, Miles had scaled no heights, and now, at forty-two, he was so afraid of them that he cowered near the steel doors of glass elevators, reluctant to move back away from them and let others step on.

"I thought we agreed you weren't going to attempt the steeple," Father Mark said.

"We did, I guess." Originally, Miles had imagined that by painting the church himself, he could save the parish a lot of money, but both contractors he'd spoken to about painting just the steeple wanted to charge nearly as much for that as they would have for the entire building. Annoyed that he proposed to do the safe, easy part himself, they let him know that the part he didn't want was the part *nobody* wanted, and that was the part that cost you. The truth of this stung. "The trouble is," Miles told his friend, "every time I look up there, it's an accusation."

"So don't look up."

"Fine advice for a man of the spirit to give," said Miles, looking up and feeling at that moment a drop of rain.

Father Mark had also looked up and also felt a drop. "Let's go over to the Rectum and have a cup of coffee," he suggested. "You can tell me about your vacation."

Ever since Miles had confessed his boyhood confusion about the words "rectory" and "rectum," Father Mark—as delighted by the mistake as Grace Roby had been—had preferred this nomenclature, even though it sometimes slipped out when it shouldn't. Such as earlier that summer when at the end of Mass he invited the parishioners to join him and Father Tom for lemonade on the lawn behind the Rectum.

St. Cat's rectory was one of Miles's favorite places. It was bright and sunny in all seasons, warm in the winter, breezy in the summer, but probably it had more to do with the fact that Father Tom—now retired but still living in the rectory—had never allowed children there. Nor had Miles's mother ever been invited in, for that matter, so perhaps it was the exclusion that added to the attraction. All of the rooms on the bottom floor were large and high-ceilinged, with tall, uncurtained windows that allowed passersby a glimpse of the privileged life inside. The Rectum's dining room, which fronted the street, had an oak dining table long enough to seat twenty guests, though when Miles and his mother walked by late on Saturday afternoons after having had their confessions heard, the room was occupied only by Father Tom, seated regally at one end, and his housekeeper, Mrs. Dumbrowski, hovering in attendance. Back then there had been two, sometimes three, priests in residence, but on Saturdays Father Tom liked to take his evening meal early and would not wait for the younger priest, who invariably drew the late confessions. Miles's mother always remarked when they passed on how sad this seemed, but Miles didn't see anything so very odd in the practice and couldn't help wondering why it so upset his mother. By the time they'd returned home, his father would already have finished eating his sandwich and departed on foot for the neighborhood tavern.

To young Miles, the forbidden rectory, so full of warmth and light and wood and books, seemed otherworldly, and he imagined that a man would have to be very rich to be a priest. The romance of the profession had stayed with him for a long time. He'd seriously considered Holy Orders well into high school, and there were still times when he wondered if he'd missed his calling. Janine had wondered too. To her way of thinking, any man with no more sex drive than Miles Roby possessed might better have just gone ahead and embraced celibacy and been done with it, instead of disappointing poor girls like herself.

Father Mark and Miles never had their coffee in the dining room he'd admired as a boy, preferring instead the kitchen with its cozy breakfast nook, a booth not unlike those along the front windows of the Empire Grill. Father Mark put a plate of cookies on the Formica table, then poured each of them a cup of coffee. Though it was only the first week in September, already autumn was in the air, rustling the lace curtains of the open window. The drizzle had stopped as soon as they entered the Rectum, but the sky remained dark. The daylight was dwindling early, giving Miles less time to work on the church. Most afternoons he managed to leave the grill by three, but by the time he changed clothes and set up the ladder, it was at least three-thirty. By six, on cloudy days, the light was failing and it was time to quit. Of course the real culprit wasn't the abbreviated day so much as the lengthening coffee conversations with Father Mark, who now slid into the booth opposite Miles. "You look like your vacation did you some good," he observed.

"It did. And there's a nice chapel in Vineyard Haven. I drove in to Mass most mornings. Tick came with me, and that was even better."

The one good thing about her parents' breakup, Tick was on record as observing, was that at least she didn't have to go to church anymore now that her mother had replaced Catholicism with aerobics. In fact, Tick considered herself an agnostic, a philosophical position that allowed her to sleep in on Sunday mornings. Miles knew better than to force her to go, and had not done so on the Vineyard, which made him even more pleased when she dragged herself out of bed, still half asleep, in the mornings to accompany him. By the time Mass was over, she was fully awake and they would enjoy a muffin together at an outdoor café before heading out-island to Peter and Dawn's house and the rest of their lazy day at the beach. Back in Maine he'd asked whether she thought she'd start going to church again now that she was back in the habit, but she didn't think so. It was easier to believe in God, she said, or at least the possibility of God, on Martha's Vineyard than it was in Empire Falls. Miles knew what she meant, understood the bitter irony. Half the cars in the Vineyard chapel's lot were either Mercedes or Lexuses. No surprise that their owners believed that God was in His heaven.

"And of course," Miles added, "Peter and Dawn spoiled her the whole time."

"Worse than you do?"

"By a mile," Miles said, chewing a cookie. Oddly, his appetite was never better than in the late afternoon here at St. Cat's. Surrounded by food all day at the restaurant, he often forgot to eat, whereas here, if he didn't pay attention, he'd finish the entire plate of cookies. "Or about as badly as I'd spoil her if I had the means. They spoiled us both, actually. Good food. A twenty-dollar bottle of wine with dinner every night."

"Must've been strange not having Janine there."

"She was invited," Miles said, surprised at the note of defensiveness in his voice.

"Never said she wasn't, Miles."

"There was plenty to occupy my thoughts without her. Their place is on a stretch of private beach, and every other woman was sunbathing in the nude. When we're not there, I suspect Peter and Dawn do too. If she had a tan line, I sure couldn't see it."

"How about Peter?" Father Mark asked. "Did *he* have a tan line?"

"Didn't occur to me to look," Miles said, smiling.

Father Mark smiled back. "Miles, you're a true Manichaean. You seek out Mass in the morning and your friend's wife's tan line in the afternoon. Anyway, what is it they do again?"

"Write television sitcoms. By next week they'll have shut everything up and flown back to L.A. You should see the house that just sits there vacant ten months out of the year."

Father Mark nodded but didn't say anything. Given the priest's political leanings, Miles knew that he didn't approve of personal wealth, much less conspicuous consumption.

"Peter said an odd thing, actually," Miles continued, even though he'd made up his mind not to tell anyone about this. "He said he and

Dawn were astonished Janine and I stuck it out as long as we did, considering how miserable we were together. They'd been admiring for years the way we kept trying to work through our problems."

Father Mark smiled. "Remember, though, people from L.A. have pretty minimal expectations when it comes to coping with marital difficulties."

Miles shrugged, conceding this. "I guess I was just surprised that people saw us that way."

"Mismatched, you mean?"

Miles considered. "Not really that so much. More that people saw us as unhappy. I *wasn't* all that unhappy . . . or I didn't know I was. So it's strange to have friends conclude something like that. I mean, if I was so unhappy, wouldn't I know?"

"Possibly," Father Mark replied. "But not necessarily."

Miles sighed. "Janine knew. I have to give her that. At least she knew how she felt."

At this point both men heard the shuffling of slippered feet in the hall. Father Mark closed his eyes, as if at the advance of a migraine. A moment later Father Tom, his gray hair wild, his collar askew, entered and fixed Miles with a particularly menacing glare.

"You want to join us, Tom?" Father Mark suggested, no doubt hoping to head off trouble. "I'll make you a cup of hot cocoa if you promise to behave."

Father Tom usually loved hot chocolate, especially when he didn't have to make it himself, but it appeared he was thirstier for a good confrontation. "Where did *that* evil bastard come from?" he growled.

Miles, also eager to placate the old priest, had been trying to get to his feet so he could offer to shake hands, but standing up proved no easy maneuver, since both the booth and the table were stationary.

"This is no evil bastard, Tom," Father Mark said calmly. "This is Miles, our most faithful parishioner. You baptized him and you married his parents."

"I know who he is," Father Tom said. "He's a peckerhead and his mother was a whore. I told her so too."

Miles sat back down. This wasn't the first time the old man, inspired by only God knew what, had taken one look at Miles and offered a poor opinion of his moral character, though he'd never before insulted the memory of Miles's mother. This was clearly an old man's dementia talking, but for the second time that afternoon Miles fleetingly considered how satisfying it would be to send another human being into the next world. This time, a priest.

"Look at him. Look at that face. He knows it's true," the old man said, taking in Miles's paint-spattered overalls. "He's a filthy degenerate is what he is. He's tracking his filth into my house."

Father Mark sighed. "You're wrong all around, Tom. First, it's not your house."

"Is too," he said.

"No, the house belongs to the parish, as you're well aware."

Father Tom seemed to consider the unfairness of this arrangement, then finally shrugged.

"And Miles isn't a degenerate," the younger priest said. "He's covered with paint because he's painting the church for us, remember? For free?"

The old man squinted first at his colleague, then at Miles. Always a frugal man in the extreme, Father Tom might have been expected to be mollified by this news, but instead he continued to glare fiercely, as if to suggest that no good deed could disguise the fundamental evil of Miles's heart. "I may be old," he conceded, "but I still know a peckerhead when I see one."

Father Mark, his patience exhausted, slid out of the booth and took him by the shoulders, rotating him gently but firmly. "Tom," he said, "look at me." When he continued to glare at Miles, Father Mark placed the tips of his fingers on the old man's stubbled chin, turning his head. "Look at me, Tom."

Finally he did, and his expression instantly morphed from disgust to shame.

"Tom," Father Mark said, "remember what we talked about before?"

If so, he showed no sign, as he studied Father Mark through red, rheumy eyes.

"I'm sorry you're not feeling well today, but this sort of behavior is intolerable. You owe our friend an apology."

To Miles, Father Tom resembled nothing more than a scolded child, convinced against his better instincts by a loving parent that he'd been a bad boy. He glanced back at Miles to see if it was possible to owe such a man an apology, then returned to Father Mark's stern gaze. The two men stared at each other long enough to make Miles squirm, but finally Father Tom turned to Miles and said, "Forgive me."

Miles didn't hesitate. "Of course, Father Tom. I'm sorry, too." And he *was* sorry. Satisfying or not, it wouldn't have been a good thing to kill an elderly priest, which also suggested it was not a good thing to wish for.

"There," Father Mark said, "that's better. Isn't it nicer for all of us when we're friends?"

Father Tom appeared to consider this extremely dubious, again studying Miles for several long beats before shaking his head and shuffling out of the room. Miles couldn't be sure, but he thought he heard one more "peckerhead" escape the old man's lips out in the hallway.

Father Mark continued to stare at the doorway as the sound of shuffling slippered feet receded. The expression on the younger priest's face wasn't quite as tolerant as one might have expected of a clergyman.

"It's okay," Miles assured him. "Father Tom and I go way back, you know. He's not himself."

"You think not?" Father Mark asked.

"It's not his fault that stuff comes out."

"True," Father Mark said. "Interesting that it's there to begin with, though. I understand why it's coming out, but how do you suppose it got *in* there?"

"Well . . ."

"I know." Father Mark grinned. "An eternal question, answered in Genesis. Still, I'm sorry he said what he did. I have no idea where he comes up with such things. He probably doesn't even remember your mother."

Miles forced himself to consider this possibility. True, the old man's mind was gone. The problem was, it wasn't completely gone, and Father Tom's eyes, especially when he was angry, often appeared to be ablaze with both intelligence and memory. "Actually, she's been on my mind lately," Miles said, adding, "I have no idea why." Though he did know. It was the Vineyard that had done it, just as it did every summer.

Outside, the rain had begun again, steadier now beneath the low sky. Miles pushed his empty coffee cup toward the center of the table.

"Well, it doesn't look like I'm painting anything today," he said, sliding out of the booth. Somehow the plate of cookies was empty, and Miles could feel the last of them lodged uncomfortably in his gullet.

Together, the two men went out onto the porch, where they stood listening to the rain.

"How many more days do you have on the north face?" Father Mark asked, contemplating the church.

"A couple," Miles said. "Maybe tomorrow and the next day if the weather clears."

"You really should stop right there," Father Mark advised. "I've been hearing more rumblings from the diocese. We may be out of business before long. I suspect poor Tom's the only thing that's saved us until now."

For more than a year now, rumors had persisted that St. Catherine's Parish would be combined with Sacred Heart, on the other side of town. Empire Falls, once sufficiently endowed with Catholics to support both, had been losing religious enthusiasm along with its population. Now the only reason for two parishes was simply that Sacré Coeur, as Sacred Heart was still known to most of its French Canadian parishioners, required a French-speaking pastor. Otherwise, the parishes could've been combined years ago. Father Mark suspected that Sacré Coeur would be the survivor and that he would be shipped elsewhere. He didn't speak French, whereas Father Tibideaux was bilingual.

What hadn't been resolved was what to do with Father Tom. While there were homes for elderly, retired priests, especially for those in ill health, his dementia, which vacillated between the obscene and the downright blasphemous, made the diocese cautious about placing him among elderly but otherwise normal clergymen, most of whom had served too long and too well to have their faith tested further in their final years by a senile old man whose favorite word was "peckerhead." Besides, Father Mark was able to handle the old priest, who had lived in St. Cat's rectory for forty years and was comfortable there. In a sense it *was* his house, just as he maintained. Also, there were words worse than "peckerhead," and if the diocese tried moving Father Tom he might start using them. Hearing him carry on had already converted several of St. Catherine's Catholics, some to Episcopalianism, a few others to fearful agnosticism, and the bishop didn't want to risk his contaminating other priests. No, the diocese seemed to believe that they had the Father Tom situation under control, and until recently they'd shown no inclination to break containment.

"Have you gotten any sense of where you might be assigned?" Miles asked.

"Not really," Father Mark said. "I suspect they're not through punishing me, though." He had a doctorate in Judaism, and the perfect position for him would be at the Newman Center of a college or university. That was the sort of post he'd held in Massachusetts before he made the mistake of joining a group of protesters who climbed the fence of a New Hampshire military installation and got arrested for whacking away at the impervious shell of a nuclear sub with ball peen hammers—an act that Father Mark had considered symbolic but that the base commander, a literalist, had interpreted as an act of sabotage and treason. Not that this protest had been Father Mark's only offense. In addition to teaching and pastoring at the university's Newman Center, Father Mark had also hosted a Sunday evening radio show, during which he had drawn his bishop's ire by counseling loving monogamy for a young male caller "regardless of the boy's sexual orientation" and further advising him to trust God's infinite understanding and mercy. Apparently, what happened to young, overeducated, rumored-to-be-gay priests who'd landed cushy campus gigs and doled out liberal advice was that they got packed off to Empire Falls, Maine, probably in hopes that God would freeze their errant peckers off.

"I hope they don't have any worse duty in mind for you," Miles said, trying to imagine what such a thing might be.

Father Mark shrugged, studying the half-painted church. "They can't really hurt you unless you let them. I certainly don't regret coming to Saint Cat's. She's been a good old gal. And I wouldn't have missed out on our friendship."

"I know," Miles said. "Me neither." Then, after a moment, "I wonder what will become of her?"

"Hard to say. Some of these beautiful old churches are being bought up and renovated into community theaters, art centers, things like that."

"I don't think that would work here," Miles said. "Empire Falls has even less interest in art than religion."

"Still, you'd better quit when you finish the north face. You could be painting Empire Falls's next Baptist church."

THE HOUSE HE GREW UP IN on Long Street had been on the market for more than a year, and Miles was parked across the street, trying to imagine what sort of person would purchase it in its present condition. The side porch, dangerous with rot even when he was a boy, had been removed but not replaced; visible evidence of where it had been wrenched away remained in four ugly, unpainted scars. Anybody who left the house by the back door, the only one Miles had ever used, would now be greeted by a six-foot drop into a patch of poisonous-looking weeds and rusted hubcaps. The rest of the structure was gray with age and neglect, its front porch sloping crazily in several different directions, as if the house had been built on a fissure. Even the FOR SALE sign on the terrace tilted.

Several different families had rented the house since his mother's death, none of them, apparently, interested in preventing or even fore-stalling its decline. Of course, to be fair, Miles had to admit that the decline had begun under the Robys' own stewardship. On what had once been a tidy, middle-class street, theirs and the Minty place next door were the first houses to prefigure the deterioration of the whole neighborhood. Miles's father, though a sometime house painter, had been disinclined to paint any house he himself happened to be living in. Summers he was busy working on the coast, and by October he would pronounce himself "all painted out," though he sometimes could be induced to work for a week or so if the landlord—with whom they had a reduced-rent arrangement contingent upon Max's keeping the house painted and in good repair—complained or threatened evic-tion. Resentful of such a strict literal interpretation of their agreement, Max retaliated by painting the house half a dozen different, largely incompatible colors from the numerous leftover, half-empty cans he'd appropriated from his various summer jobs. The Roby cellar was always full of stacked gallon cans, their lids slightly askew, the damp, rotting shelves full of open mason jars of turpentine, the fumes from which permeated the upstairs throughout the winter. Miles was in fourth grade when one of his friends asked what it was like to live in the joke house, a remark he passed along not to his father, who was respon-sible for its harlequin appearance, but to his mother, who first flushed crimson, then looked as if she might burst into tears, then ran into her bedroom, slammed the door and did. Later, red-eyed, she explained to Miles that what was on the inside of a house (love, she seemed to have in mind) was more important than what was on the outside (paint, preferably in one hue), but after Miles went to bed he heard his parents arguing, and after that night Max never painted the house again. Now its motley color scheme had weathered into uniform gray.

Miles hadn't been parked across the street for more than a minute, staring up at the dark, shadeless window of the room where his mother had begun her death march, before a police car wheeled around the corner two blocks up Long and came toward him, swerving across the street and rocking to a halt so close that its bumper was mere inches from the Jetta's own grill. A young policeman was at the wheel, one Miles didn't recognize, and when he got out of the cruiser, putting on sunglasses that the gloomy sky didn't warrant, Miles rolled down his window.

"License and registration," the young cop said.

"Is there a problem, officer?"

"License and registration," the cop repeated, his tone a little harder this time.

Miles fished the registration out of the glove box and handed it out the window along with his license. The policeman attached both to the top of his clipboard and made a couple notes.

"You mind telling me what you're doing here, Mr. Roby?"

"Yes, I do," said Miles, who would have been reluctant to even if he'd had an explanation that made any sense. That a demented priest had called his mother a whore, thereby compelling him to visit the house he'd grown up in, as if his mother, dead these twenty years, might be rocking on the porch, did not strike Miles as the sort of story that would satisfy a man who felt compelled to wear sunglasses on dark, rainy afternoons.

"Why's that, Mr. Roby?"

To Miles, this didn't sound like a serious question, so he didn't answer it.

The young policeman scratched some more on his form. "Maybe you didn't hear the question?" he finally said.

"Have I done something illegal?"

Now it was the cop's turn to fall silent. For a full minute he ignored Miles, apparently to prove that he too could play this silence game. "Are you aware that you're driving an unregistered vehicle, Mr. Roby?"

"I believe you have the registration in your hand."

"Expired last month."

"I'll have to take care of it."

The cop didn't register this remark, instead pointing at the inspection sticker on the windshield. "Your inspection's also past due."

"I guess I'll have to take care of that, too."

No opinion on this either. "So what are you doing here, Mr. Roby?" the officer said, as if he were asking this question for the first time.

"I used to live in that house," Miles said, indicating which one.

"Used to. But not now."

"That's right."

Miles then caught a glimpse of something red in his rearview mirror and turned in time to see Jimmy Minty's red Camaro pulling up behind him. Jimmy, who'd grown up next door, was about the last person Miles would have wanted to catch him parked just here. When Jimmy rolled down his window, the young cop abruptly walked back to the Camaro. Miles watched their conversation in the mirror, smiling when the officer took off his dark glasses. In such situations, apparently only the ranking officer got to keep his glasses on. The conversation was short, then Jimmy Minty did a U-turn and headed back down the street in the direction he'd come from. The young officer, clearly disappointed, watched him go, then returned to Miles and handed back his license and registration. "Might be a good idea to take care of these today," he said, the confrontational edge gone from his voice now.

"You're not citing me?"

"Not unless you think I should, Mr. Roby."

Miles put the license back in his wallet, the registration back in the glove compartment.

Now that they were pals, the cop seemed anxious that there should be no hard feelings. "You lived in that house there?"

Miles nodded, slipping the Jetta in gear.

"Huh," the young cop said. "Looks haunted."

THE MOTOR VEHICLES DIVISION office was being run out of the Whiting mansion, or rather "the Cottage," a large outbuilding nestled in a grove of trees behind the main house. This arrangement was only temporary, until renovations at the courthouse, whose domed roof had partially collapsed after last winter's ice storm, were completed. Since then, justice—never swift in Empire Falls—had ground to a virtual halt. Except for traffic court, most legal matters were being processed out of nearby Fairhaven, whose docket had grown so crowded with the legal business of both towns that everything from building permits to property disputes to small claims to assessments was backed up for months. Even the simplest legal transactions, like Miles's uncontested divorce, seemed endlessly bogged down. Since he hadn't wanted the divorce to begin with, he wasn't terribly troubled. In fact, last spring he'd hoped the holdup might cause Janine to reconsider, though by now he knew that she was determined to marry the Silver Fox, and that somehow she held this legal delay, which had ruined her plans for a summer wedding, against Miles. So determined was she to marry Walt Comeau the moment her divorce became final that Miles had begun to suspect that in some part of her brain, the workings of which still mystified him, Janine realized that this second marriage was some pure folly she needed to commit quickly, lest she come to her senses first.

Miles parked in the small lot between the main house, now headquarters of the Dexter County Museum and Historical Society, and the cottage, which housed, in addition to the temporary DMV, the permanent offices of the Empire Falls Planning and Development Commission, which over the last decade had become something of a joke, since no one had developed anything in Empire Falls during that period, nor was anyone planning to. Mrs. Whiting, as director of the board, kept an office there, however, and when Miles saw her Lincoln parked in the lot, he hurried across the lawn, head down, in the hope that she wouldn't spy him out her window. He'd been avoiding "the State of the Grill" since his return from vacation, and despite the restaurant's improved business, he was even more reluctant than usual to spend an afternoon going over receipts and making projections.

Safely inside, he joined a short line and awaited his turn at a window marked AUTO REG. The entire mahogany counter, he realized, had been transported from the courthouse, and would no doubt be ferried back again. The other furnishings, including the paintings and photographs of Whiting males that decorated the walls, all belonged to the museum collection. Miles studied these men while he waited. For direct lineal descendants they didn't look all that much alike except, Miles decided, for one feature. Even as young men, they appeared prematurely old, or maybe just distinguished, their hair white, their brows chiseled in cogitation. Or perhaps they were reflecting with satisfaction that the history of Empire Falls, indeed of Dexter County, was little more than the history of their own family.

After a few minutes, he noticed Jimmy Minty's red Camaro pull into the lot. Leaving the car idling, the police officer got out and came toward the cottage, angling off the walkway that led to Motor Vehicles and proceeding across the lawn to the back of the building. Miles followed his progress until a man behind him in line tapped him on the shoulder and pointed out that it was his turn. At the window he wrote out the check for his new tags and slipped it through the opening. When the woman on the other side of the glass smiled and said, "Hello, Miles," he recognized her as a girl he'd gone to high school with. Marcia, according to her name tag. Which was more likely, he wondered, that he and Marcia should have lived so long in such a small town without running into each other, or that he and Jimmy Minty would cross paths twice in half an hour?

"You keep this car another year or two and we'll have to pay *you* to register it," the clerk observed when she saw the amount of the check he'd written out.

"That would be fine with me, Marcia," Miles told her, hoping she'd conclude that he'd remembered her name across the long span of years.

"Here's your new chickadee plates," she said, pushing a pair through the opening.

"What was wrong with the lobster ones?"

"People from out of state made fun of them. Said the lobsters looked like cockroaches."

Miles studied the new plates, which didn't strike him as much of an improvement, though the lobsters *had* looked like cockroaches. "I hope this doesn't mean we have to start eating chickadees."

"It may come to that, if things don't start looking up," she said. "I hear there might be a buyer for the mill, though."

Miles considered asking where she'd heard this. After all, the Planning and Development Commission office was only a few feet away, so it was possible she might have overheard something genuine. More likely, however, was that she'd overheard somebody standing in this very line, somebody who'd had coffee that morning at the Empire Grill.

Through another window Jimmy Minty could now be seen standing on the doorstep of the Empire Falls Planning and Development Commission office, conversing with someone who, because of the angle, wasn't visible, though Miles immediately concluded that it had to be Mrs. Whiting. The policeman's body language told the story; he was listening with much the same attitude as the younger policeman had listened to *him* half an hour earlier, and this time it was Minty who removed his dark glasses. Miles watched as he nodded once, twice, three times, apparently at specific instructions. Was it Miles's imagination, or did Minty glance quickly into the Motor Vehicles office and then away again, as if he'd been told not to?

"Don't you think?" Marcia was saying.

"I'm sorry," Miles said, returning his attention to her. "Don't I think what?"

somehow she held this legal delay, which had ruined her plans for a summer wedding, against Miles. So determined was she to marry Walt Comeau the moment her divorce became final that Miles had begun to suspect that in some part of her brain, the workings of which still mystified him, Janine realized that this second marriage was some pure folly she needed to commit quickly, lest she come to her senses first.

Miles parked in the small lot between the main house, now headquarters of the Dexter County Museum and Historical Society, and the cottage, which housed, in addition to the temporary DMV, the permanent offices of the Empire Falls Planning and Development Commission, which over the last decade had become something of a joke, since no one had developed anything in Empire Falls during that period, nor was anyone planning to. Mrs. Whiting, as director of the board, kept an office there, however, and when Miles saw her Lincoln parked in the lot, he hurried across the lawn, head down, in the hope that she wouldn't spy him out her window. He'd been avoiding "the State of the Grill" since his return from vacation, and despite the restaurant's improved business, he was even more reluctant than usual to spend an afternoon going over receipts and making projections.

Safely inside, he joined a short line and awaited his turn at a window marked AUTO REG. The entire mahogany counter, he realized, had been transported from the courthouse, and would no doubt be ferried back again. The other furnishings, including the paintings and photographs of Whiting males that decorated the walls, all belonged to the museum collection. Miles studied these men while he waited. For direct lineal descendants they didn't look all that much alike except, Miles decided, for one feature. Even as young men, they appeared prematurely old, or maybe just distinguished, their hair white, their brows chiseled in cogitation. Or perhaps they were reflecting with satisfaction that the history of Empire Falls, indeed of Dexter County, was little more than the history of their own family.

After a few minutes, he noticed Jimmy Minty's red Camaro pull into the lot. Leaving the car idling, the police officer got out and came toward the cottage, angling off the walkway that led to Motor Vehicles and proceeding across the lawn to the back of the building. Miles followed his progress until a man behind him in line tapped him on the shoulder and pointed out that it was his turn. At the window he wrote out the check for his new tags and slipped it through the opening. When the woman on the other side of the glass smiled and said, "Hello, Miles," he recognized her as a girl he'd gone to high school with. Marcia, according to her name tag. Which was more likely, he wondered, that he and Marcia should have lived so long in such a small town without running into each other, or that he and Jimmy Minty would cross paths twice in half an hour?

"You keep this car another year or two and we'll have to pay *you* to register it," the clerk observed when she saw the amount of the check he'd written out.

"That would be fine with me, Marcia," Miles told her, hoping she'd conclude that he'd remembered her name across the long span of years.

"Here's your new chickadee plates," she said, pushing a pair through the opening.

"What was wrong with the lobster ones?"

"People from out of state made fun of them. Said the lobsters looked like cockroaches."

Miles studied the new plates, which didn't strike him as much of an improvement, though the lobsters *had* looked like cockroaches. "I hope this doesn't mean we have to start eating chickadees."

"It may come to that, if things don't start looking up," she said. "I hear there might be a buyer for the mill, though."

Miles considered asking where she'd heard this. After all, the Planning and Development Commission office was only a few feet away, so it was possible she might have overheard something genuine. More likely, however, was that she'd overheard somebody standing in this very line, somebody who'd had coffee that morning at the Empire Grill.

Through another window Jimmy Minty could now be seen standing on the doorstep of the Empire Falls Planning and Development Commission office, conversing with someone who, because of the angle, wasn't visible, though Miles immediately concluded that it had to be Mrs. Whiting. The policeman's body language told the story; he was listening with much the same attitude as the younger policeman had listened to *him* half an hour earlier, and this time it was Minty who removed his dark glasses. Miles watched as he nodded once, twice, three times, apparently at specific instructions. Was it Miles's imagination, or did Minty glance quickly into the Motor Vehicles office and then away again, as if he'd been told not to?

"Don't you think?" Marcia was saying.

"I'm sorry," Miles said, returning his attention to her. "Don't I think what?"

"I said it's about time our luck changed around here."

"It sure is," Miles agreed. Assuming it's luck that's the problem, of course. Which he privately doubted. The problem with trying to gauge mathematical probability was that it presupposed the circumstance you were observing was governed by chance.

Outside, Jimmy Minty nodded one last time before recrossing the lawn to his idling Camaro and pulling back out onto Empire Avenue. Miles waited until he'd turned the corner before tucking his new license plates under his arm and heading for the door. Before he could complete his escape, though, Marcia's phone rang and he heard her say, "Yes, it is," and then call his name. He thought he might just keep going, pretending not to hear. Then he thought again.

MRS. WHITING was on the phone when he knocked and entered, but she acknowledged his presence by pointing to a chair. Miles, however, was reluctant to sit down before scanning the room for the old woman's frequent companion, a vicious black cat named Timmy. Miles was allergic to cats in general and Mrs. Whiting's in particular. It was a rare encounter between the two that didn't leave Miles striped and puffy.

Mrs. Whiting smiled and put her hand over the phone. "You can relax," she assured him. "I left Timmy at home."

"Are you sure?" Miles wondered, still far from at ease. The cat in question, in Miles's opinion, possessed many borderline supernatural abilities, including a talent for materializing at will.

"That's hilarious, dear boy," she replied, then resumed her conversation on the phone. Their twenty-year relationship, Miles often thought, could be summed up in those four words. From the beginning, when Miles and her daughter, Cindy, were in high school together, Mrs. Whiting had referred to him as "dear boy," though Miles doubted he was particularly dear to her. And she was forever pronouncing things he said "hilarious," despite a demeanor that suggested she didn't find them even remotely funny.

The Planning and Development Commission office, which Miles had never entered before, was large, and along one whole wall sat a scale model of downtown Empire Falls, so obviously idealized that he didn't immediately recognize it as the town he'd lived his whole life in. The streets were lined with bright green toy trees, and the buildings so brightly painted, the streets so clean, that Miles's first thought was that this was an artist's notion of what a future Empire Falls might look like after an ambitious and costly revitalization project. Only closer inspection revealed that the model represented not the future but the past. This, Miles realized, was the Empire Falls of his own childhood, and he noticed several businesses along Empire Avenue that had been razed over the last two decades, leaving in real life a rash of excess parking lots. The Empire Grill, neglected in real life, in miniature looked as if Mrs. Whiting had given Miles every penny he'd ever asked for.

A small silver plate on the base read: "EMPIRE FALLS, CIRCA 1959." The actual town, of course, had never looked quite so prosperous. Even in 1959 the brick walls of the textile mill and the shirt factory— bright red on the model—had gone rust brown, even black in some places, with weather and soot. And the river that ran past them on the model had been rendered sky blue. Now *that's* hilarious, Miles thought. Surely the only time in the last hundred years that the Knox had run blue was when the textile mill was dumping blue dye into it. Even more hilarious was the idea that such a nostalgic past should have found a home in the town's planning and development office. Evidently the commission's plan was to turn back the clock.

Elijah Whiting, whose stern portrait overlooked the model, failed to see the humor in any of this. Like the Whitings in the other room, old Elijah wore a grim expression, and he had the same weakness about the mouth. They all reminded Miles of someone, though he couldn't imagine who.

When Mrs. Whiting said good-bye and hung up, she did it so perfunctorily that Miles couldn't help wondering whether she'd really been on the phone or was just using the pretense to study him. Around her, this feeling of being scrutinized was not unusual. She now rotated in her chair, leaned back and regarded Elijah Whiting. "They were all mad as hatters, you know. In one way or another. You can see it lurking behind the eyes, if you look."

Miles did look, though he didn't see what he was supposed to. There was a quality of zealousness perhaps, of bigotry maybe, but not of insanity.

"You probably heard the stories about this distinguished ancestor when you were a boy?"

"I don't think so."

"He's said to have chased his wife around this very room with a shovel, intent on bashing in her skull."

"Surely nothing like that ever happened *here*," Miles said, indicating the model, in which only the Whiting estate didn't look different in quality from its appearance in real life. It suddenly occurred to Miles that Mrs. Whiting herself must have commissioned it. By idealizing the rest of the town, she had successfully obscured the truth—that its wealth and vitality had been bled dry by the generations of a single family. A cynical interpretation, perhaps, but it also explained why the house C. B. Whiting had built across the river was not represented on the model at all. Across the Iron Bridge was virgin wilderness, all lush trees and rolling hills.

"Seeing you standing there gives me an inspiration," the old woman said, though Miles doubted, even before she continued, that her sudden intuition would be anything like his own. "You should be mayor."

"Of the model?" Miles smiled. "I could just about afford that." Being mayor of Empire Falls was a full-time job with a part-time salary, though it was often remarked that past mayors had found ways to supplement their income.

"You're too modest, dear boy. I've often thought you should run for political office."

Miles decided not to remind her that he'd run for school board twice and been elected.

"Are you offering me the job?"

"You overestimate the extent of my influence, dear boy." She smiled. "You're rather like your mother in that respect. But then, people are forever confusing will with power, don't you find? I have a theory about why, if you're interested."

"Why I'm like my mother," Miles asked, finally taking his seat, "or why people confuse will with power?"

"The latter," she said. "After all, there's nothing very mysterious about why you take after your mother, is there. Your father isn't exactly the sort of man who inspires imitation. No, people confuse power with will because so few of them have the foggiest idea what they want. Absent any knowledge, will remains impotent. A limp dick, as it were." She regarded him, eyebrow arched. "The lucky few who happen actually to know what they want are said to have will-*power*."

"That's all it takes?"

"Well, let's call it a necessary beginning."

Miles allowed himself to settle into his chair. More than anyone he knew, Mrs. Whiting had the ability to draw him into conversations he otherwise would have avoided. The reason seemed to be that her conclusions were invariably antithetical to his own. "So you think human beings are meant to know what they want?"

Mrs. Whiting sighed. "That word 'meant' suggests you're up to your old tricks, dear boy, casting everything in a religious light. That won't do if you intend to be mayor."

"I don't," he pointed out. "Certainly not of Empire Falls in 1959."

"But that's where you're foolish, dear boy. Most Americans *want* it to be 1959, with the addition of cappuccino and cable TV."

"That's what they want, or what they *think* they want?" The person he was thinking of was Janine. His soon-to-be-ex-wife was never uncertain about what she wanted, just disappointed by its eventual acquisition. Miles himself had been an example. The Silver Fox, though he didn't yet suspect it, would be another.

"That's not a particularly helpful distinction, is it? What is wanting but thinking? But for the sake of argument, let's accept your terms and begin at the beginning. Adam and Eve. They knew what *they* wanted, did they not?"

"I doubt it," Miles said, also for the sake of argument. "Until it was forbidden."

"Precisely, dear boy. But once it was forbidden, they suffered no such doubts—am I correct?"

"No. Just regrets."

"Do you imagine that refusing the forbidden fruit would've made them happier? Would *that* have eliminated regret or merely re-defined it?"

She had a point. "I guess we'll never know."

"*I* certainly won't, dear boy, but like our progenitors, I've not re-sisted many temptations. *You*, on the other hand . . ." She dangled the thought. Mrs. Whiting had never made any secret that she considered Miles a case study in repression. "Did you have a nice vacation?"

"Wonderful," he said, eager for the old woman to understand that fine times could be had by others.

Mrs. Whiting studied him carefully, as if suspicious that his enthu-siasm masked a falsehood. "You return there every summer, don't you."

"Just about."

"Has it occurred to you to wonder why?"

"No," he told her. When not insinuating that he was repressed, the old woman liked to imply that despite his intelligence, his views were parochial, the result of his having traveled and seen so little. Like many rich people, she seemed not to understand why the poor didn't think to winter in Capri, where the weather was more clement. Nor did it strike her as unfair to suggest as much to a man who for twenty years had tended one of her businesses while *she* traveled. "I've got friends who have a house there," he continued, leaving unsaid what Mrs. Whiting no doubt understood perfectly well—that only charity made even so modest a vacation possible.

Actually, it was Miles who had introduced Peter and Dawn to the Vineyard all those years ago, during college. They'd all been poor then, and when they pooled their resources that fall they'd had just about enough to pay for the ferry crossing. They'd slept on the beach, illegally, beneath the cliffs at Gay Head, confident that after Labor Day they wouldn't be rousted by the island police, who probably numbered no more than half a dozen. It was during this weekend on the island, Miles suspected, that Peter and Dawn had fallen in love, first with the island and then with each other. Since then they'd considered Miles instrumental to their happiness and were grateful to him for it. Even if their affection for each other had begun to wear thin, as he feared, clearly they both still loved the Vineyard. He couldn't imagine either one of them conceding the house in a divorce settlement.

"Yes, well, that makes sense," Mrs. Whiting grudgingly acknowledged. "And yet—"

"And yet what?"

She appeared to lose her train of thought, but only momentarily. "And yet 'we beat on, boats against the current, borne back ceaselessly into the past.'" The old woman was smiling at him knowingly, and Miles, who recognized the final line of *The Great Gatsby*, felt an intense obligation to reveal neither this nor the slightest curiosity about her intention.

When the phone rang, both were visibly relieved. Mrs. Whiting picked up the receiver and waved good-bye in one efficient motion, dismissing Miles without further ceremony.

A hell of a way, Miles thought, to treat someone you'd just encouraged to run for mayor.

CHAPTER 3

W HEN JANINE FINISHED her last aerobics class, she showered quickly and drove over to the Empire Grill, circling the block to make sure Miles wasn't there. Even though the divorce was dragging on forever, the whole thing had been amicable enough. In fact, she'd liked Miles better these last nine months since they'd decided to separate than at any time in the previous twenty years. Still, she had no desire to see him right now, especially not in the company of her fiancé. It was genuinely weird the way Walt had begun hanging out at the grill, a place he'd totally avoided when they were sneaking around.

Pulling in and parking next to Walt's van, she made a point of not looking at the stenciled logo, not wanting to admit that it was beginning to irritate her. THE SILVER FOX. What sort of man would write that on his car? For Janine this question was neither idle nor rhetorical. She was going to marry Walt Comeau as soon as the divorce was final, and part of her wanted to know the answer to that question before she became half owner of the vehicle and sole owner of the driver.

Then again, some questions were better left unanswered. She knew Walt pretty well, certainly better than she'd known Miles. Back when they got married, she hadn't even known who *she* was, her own self, never mind her intended. At least now Janine knew who Janine was, what Janine wanted, and, just as important, what Janine didn't want. She didn't want Miles, or anyone who reminded her of Miles. She didn't want to be fat anymore, either. Never, ever, again. Also, she wanted a real sex life, and she wanted to act young for a change, something she hadn't been able to do when she actually was young. She wanted to dance and have men look at her. She liked the way her body felt after dropping all that weight, and by God she liked to come. For Janine, at forty, orgasms were a new thing and she damn near lost her mind every time she had another, or when she contemplated how close she'd come to going her whole life without experiencing that singular, incomparable, tingling, explosive, mind-bending thrill. The first one had so caught her by surprise that at the height of the wave she went someplace very far away, then returned, sobbing in Walt's arms, having concluded she'd never get to go there again, though he assured her she would and then made sure that she did. Damn, she remembered thinking. I mean, *DAMN*.

It was Walt Comeau who'd taught her about herself and her body's needs, though she was beginning to realize that even Walt's views on the matter were oversimplified. To his way of thinking, what her body needed was lots of exercise and lots of Walt. Janine herself was wondering if her body might not benefit from a little travel. She didn't mind working out at Walt's own club, but she'd read somewhere about a spa out in the desert near Tucson, Arizona, that specialized in women's bodies. "Luxurious" was the word the brochure used, and now that Janine was beginning to feel luxurious about her body she thought she deserved a week or two at a place like that. It was expensive, sure, but Walt was always going on about all his money, and she kept hoping to talk him into honeymooning there. And once Tick graduated from high school, what would prevent them from relocating to a warmer climate? After living in Maine all her life, it'd be nice to be someplace where the sun came out and stayed out. Walt was always talking about opening up a new health club, so why not Sedona or Santa Fe? If what she heard was true, the desert Southwest was like California. People kept fit and healthy and wore bathing suits that were basically symbolic of clothing. If Walt didn't want to at least check it out, Janine wouldn't mind going by herself for a week. She'd liked the look of the Latino masseurs in the brochure. Which seemed a little ungrateful, she had to admit. After all, Walt had been the one who woke her up, who helped her locate herself, the person she really was. And he also located that wonderful spot, found it right away, the one Miles never suspected the existence of. Now here she was thinking about Latino masseurs.

If only he just hadn't stenciled those stupid words on the side of the van, Janine thought as she got out of her Blazer. Probably "stupid" wasn't the right spin. They weren't stupid so much as boastful, she decided, heading for the front door of the restaurant. Besides, wasn't it Walt's cockiness that had attracted her in the first place? The fact that he was so different from Miles, who was so docile? Her mother, of course, still loved Miles and sided with him on all occasions, referring to Walt as "that little banty rooster." "Miles is modest for good reason, Ma, believe me," she assured her mother. A mean thing to say, maybe, but true, and it hinted at what there was no way to discuss with Bea— the whole sex thing. Her mother, Janine felt certain, was one of those poor women who'd managed to do what Janine herself had damn near done. She'd lived her entire adult life from one end to the other without a single orgasm. When Bea died, it would be possible to say truthfully that she went before she came. Not Janine. If she'd been the sort of person to stencil anything on the side of a van, it'd be something more like, SHE CAME BEFORE SHE WENT. Which meant, she supposed, that she and Walt Comeau were made for each other, and she ought to quit thinking about the strong hands of Latino masseurs.

"Hey, babe," she said, sliding onto a stool next to the man she'd be married to next month, if her idiot lawyer was to be believed. Unless the roof of the Fairhaven courthouse fell in too, which wouldn't surprise Janine one bit, not the way everything had been conspiring against her right from the start, when she made the mistake of telling that priest with the Alzheimer's all about herself and Walt, figuring he'd forgive her and then forget all about it. Everyone said he couldn't remember twice around, which was why they'd finally had to hire the younger priest. Except that this time the old guy remembered three or four times around. He told Miles everything she'd said in the confessional and then, forgetting he'd told him, told him again the next day.

Still, now that it was almost over, Janine figured it was probably just as well the old nitwit had squealed on her. At the time she'd been confused about what she wanted, or else she wouldn't have gone to a priest at all. Once everything was out in the open, it occurred to her that what she wanted was Walt and for the two of them to make up for all the sex she'd been cheated out of. If that meant everybody thought she was a slut, including her daughter and her own mother, then they could just think whatever they wanted. In a sense it was good she and Walt got caught, because if they hadn't, Walt, being a man, probably would've been just as happy to keep on with the hanky-panky. It was Janine who hadn't liked all the sneaking around, and getting caught had at least set the legal ball rolling, which was something. Keeping it rolling had required all her energy, except for what she kept in reserve for sex and the Stairmaster. The last nine months had proved one thing beyond a shadow of a doubt: you can't beat city hall the same year its roof falls in.

Walt was intently playing gin with Horace, so he didn't notice when she came in. Another thing that was beginning to bother Janine was the way Walt knitted his brow over anything that taxed his intellect. Quite a lot did, Janine had to admit, so she had plenty of opportunity to study her least favorite expression. Walt was wearing it now as he looked up from his hand to study his opponent, as if the solution to whatever perplexed him might scroll across Horace's broad forehead, disgusting cyst and all. At moments like this, his brow tightly knit, his eyes narrowed, Walt Comeau always looked like he was trying to figure out not how his opponent happened to be winning so much as how he was cheating, and Janine wondered if this sly, distrustful expression might be responsible for his nickname. Certainly it always made Janine want to take him aside and explain exactly how he was being cheated. "He's smarter than you, Walt," she'd have liked to tell him. "He's cheating you by remembering what cards you've played and what cards he's played. That's how he knows what's left in the deck. He pays attention to what you're doing, and to what it means. It's not a damn marked deck, and he doesn't have an accomplice, and there's no mirror behind you reflecting your cards. He's just smarter than you. It might not be fair, but he is."

Miles, bad as *he* was, had been a far better card partner. He had no poker face at all, and he couldn't help looking surprised when Lady Luck smiled on him and disappointed when she didn't, but at least he was more often a step ahead of the game than a step behind, like the Silver Fox. To Janine, one of life's crueler ironies was that Miles, who often could locate the Queen of Spades two tricks into a game of hearts, hadn't been able to find her spot in twenty years of marriage.

Janine counted Mississippis and got to ten before Walt decided what to discard, which ginned Horace nicely. Walt, ever curious, turned over the card Horace had laid facedown, groaning when he saw what it was. "You lucky bastard," he said. "That was *my* damn gin card."

"I knew that, Mr. Comeau," Horace explained, totaling up the points he'd caught Walt with. "Why do you suppose I wouldn't give it to you?"

Thus released from his torment, Walt rotated on his stool and took in the woman who would soon be his wife, breaking into a wide grin.

This, Janine realized as Walt looked her over, was why she was marrying the man. He might be a beat slow—all right, several beats slow—but damn if he wasn't always glad to see her. He always drank her in with what seemed to be fresh eyes, and she didn't really care if the reason for this might be short-term memory deficiency. Walt's appreciation made her glow inside, opening her up, allowing her spot to unfold like the soft petals of a flower so obviously that even Miles could have found it, not that he'd ever have the opportunity again. "Hey, good-lookin'," Walt said. "Good thing Big Boy isn't here. He'd commit hari-kari seeing how good you look."

Having given voice to this pleasantly dark thought, Walt turned to Horace for a second opinion. "How'd you like to go through the rest of your life knowing you had a woman this beautiful and lost her?"

Horace was either still totaling up their score on his notepad or pretending to, forcing Walt to rotate back on his stool. "Let me guess," he said. "One twenty-two."

Well, sure, okay. Here was another thing that irritated Janine, this constant public guessing game about her weight. Not that she wasn't proud of having dropped the fifty pounds. And she knew, too, that Walt did it because he was proud of her. Still, it reminded her a little of that midway trick back when she was a girl, the booth where they guessed people's weights. "One twenty-three." Pleased in spite of herself, she grinned at him. "But can we *not* have this conversation in public?"

"One twenty-*three*?" Walt bellowed. "I'm going to get that scale in the women's locker room checked out." Again he rotated on his stool and nudged Horace. "How about it, though? One twenty-three. Guess how much she weighed when we met."

"I'd be *real* careful," Janine advised Horace, who looked like he didn't need to be warned.

"Don't be like that," Walt said. "You should be proud." Then, rotating back to Horace, "Mid one-eighties."

"You want anything, Janine?" David called over his shoulder from where he was browning a roast. Without, of course, actually looking at her.

"No, I'm fine," she told him. "Tick almost done back there?"

"Pretty close." Still not looking up from his work, the prick.

"Tell her I'm here, okay?"

"She knows you're here."

The implication being what—that the kid could smell it when she came in? Or that Janine's appearance altered the whole atmosphere?

"Can you believe this woman?" Walt now asked. "No, I sure wouldn't want to be that brother of yours, knowing I let a woman this good-looking get away from me."

"She's a beauty, all right," David agreed.

"Hear that?" Walt said, nuzzling Janine's neck. "Everybody says the same thing."

Janine had heard what her brother-in-law said—heard it a lot clearer than the Silver Fox had, and she leaned away from his cold nose. At home she might've enjoyed the affection, but not here, especially with people making sarcastic remarks. To show David who was boss, she got up and went around the counter to the register, hit No Sale, and the drawer flew open.

"I'm changing a fifty here, David," she called. "That all right with you? Since I'm a former employee and all-around beauty queen?"

"If it's all right with Miles," he said. "I just work here."

Which pissed her off even more. "You can come over and watch if you want."

Charlene stepped up just then, snatched the fifty, and quickly made change out of the drawer, then slammed it by way of punctuation. "How you doin', Janine?"

"Just fine, Charl." She wadded up the bills and stuffed them in her purse, feeling robbed of some vague satisfaction. She hadn't needed change for the fifty to begin with. The good news, she thought, watching Charlene arranging tables for tonight's private party, was that, at forty-five, Charlene was finally showing her age. Since her operation she looked tired, and a little fan of lines had appeared at the corners of her eyes and was deepening there. By the look of her, she'd also put on about ten pounds, which made Janine wonder how much longer her soon-to-be-ex-husband would continue mooning over her. That would be a hard habit for him to break, having been at it his entire married life. In matters of the heart, Miles was even more transparent than when he was playing cards. When it came to what he was holding close to his vest, he'd just hang on to it, tight as grim death, and deny it was there, no matter how hard you tried to pry it out of him.

When Charlene finished rearranging tables, Janine couldn't help but smile. Another year or two and that's going to be one fat ass, lady, she thought. Drape it with a sheet and show home movies. This last weekend, Janine had noticed, the college boys returning for the fall semester hadn't been quite as flirtatious, and this year they actually seemed more interested in their own dates than in peeking down Charlene's shirt. Next year, even the salesmen who pushed dollies full of canned goods into the back, calling out mock invitations for her to join them in the walk-in cooler for a minute, would stop treating her like she was sex on the hoof. And then that would leave just Miles in love with her—and not really her, either, but the woman she was before she wore out, the woman he still believed her to be, against the testimony of his own eyes.

There, Janine thought. Now I've thoroughly depressed myself. Because the truth was, she liked Charlene, who'd had four bad marriages and her own share of heartache, and never once during the years that Janine and Miles were married had she encouraged his crush, any more than she encouraged the college boys. It was her body that drew them, and she couldn't help that. While it was pleasurable to consider that Janine was winning her own body war at about the same rate that Charlene was losing hers, Janine was too smart not to see the end of all this, which was that they would both lose. The competition for the love and admiration of men like Walt and Miles would be passed like a torch to some other girl, some kid, really, who'd look at Janine and Charlene and never even suspect that they'd been there and done that. The sad, fucking truth was that no matter who you are, you never, ever, will get your fill.

In full possession of this wisdom, Janine slipped her left hand beneath the counter and into the front trouser pocket of the Silver Fox, who smiled slyly and slowly rose to the occasion. That Walt was fifty *did* worry her a little. She was getting started late, orgasm-wise, and it'd be just her luck for Walt to shut down early. He wasn't exactly leaping to attention at the moment, but he was getting there.

Down at the other end of the restaurant there was a table full of young women from the Dexter County Academy of Hair Design who came in most afternoons a few minutes before closing and hunkered down in the far booth, chattering and whispering and eating pie. Studying these girls, she wondered if one of them might be the next Charlene, the next Janine. A couple were almost pretty if you imagined them without the big hair and the extra pounds that already, in their early twenties, were weighing them down. No, maybe Janine's days, like Charlene's, were numbered, but at least there didn't seem to be much competition on the immediate horizon, which meant that for a while she'd have the field, such as it was, to herself.

Janine was smiling when the door to the kitchen swung open and her daughter appeared, announcing that she was ready to go home.

Walt, apparently forgetting there was a friendly hand in his front trouser pocket, damn near leapt off his stool, twisting Janine's wrist in the process. "*There* she is," he cried, ignoring his fiancée's distress. "There's our little beauty."

IN ART CLASS, the five long, rectangular tables are all color-coded, seven or eight students at each, and Tick has been assigned to Blue. Mrs. Roderigue, the art teacher, is a large woman with a massive shelf of a bosom, of which she appears to have no knowledge. When she enters the classroom and one of the boys says, all too audibly, "Bah-zoooom!," she never seems to connect her own appearance with this too predictable utterance. Though Mrs. Roderigue is about Tick's father's age, she seems older, perhaps because she wears her hair in a style that Tick associates only with elderly women.

As a teacher, what Mrs. Roderigue prides herself most on is her organization. "There are forty of you," she told the class after they were all seated that first day, "and so it will be imperative that we *get* organized and *stay* organized." Normally classes are not allowed to grow so large, but an exception is made for art—unspoken acknowledgment, Tick suspects, that nobody considers art to be a real course, like history or math. Mrs. Roderigue isn't even full-time, teaching afternoons at the high school, mornings at the middle school, her teaching strategies identical regardless of her audience.

For Tick, the interesting thing about Mrs. Roderigue's color coding is that the tables themselves are all steel gray, so the only way to differentiate Blue from Red that first day was to read the signs—BLUE, GREEN, RED, YELLOW and BROWN, carefully lettered in black ink—taped to each. On the second day all the signs came down and were slipped into plastic baggies before they could be dirtied or wrinkled. Art, she told her students, was the study and practice of order. There was no such thing as Sloppy Art. Artists, she claimed, first had to know where much competition on the immediate horizon, which meant that for a while she'd have the field, such as it was, to herself.

Janine was smiling when the door to the kitchen swung open and her daughter appeared, announcing that she was ready to go home.

Walt, apparently forgetting there was a friendly hand in his front trouser pocket, damn near leapt off his stool, twisting Janine's wrist in the process. "*There* she is," he cried, ignoring his fiancée's distress. "There's our little beauty."

I N ART CLASS, the five long, rectangular tables are all color-coded, seven or eight students at each, and Tick has been assigned to Blue. Mrs. Roderigue, the art teacher, is a large woman with a massive shelf of a bosom, of which she appears to have no knowledge. When she enters the classroom and one of the boys says, all too audibly, "Bah-zoooom!," she never seems to connect her own appearance with this too predictable utterance. Though Mrs. Roderigue is about Tick's father's age, she seems older, perhaps because she wears her hair in a style that Tick associates only with elderly women.

As a teacher, what Mrs. Roderigue prides herself most on is her organization. "There are forty of you," she told the class after they were all seated that first day, "and so it will be imperative that we *get* organized and *stay* organized." Normally classes are not allowed to grow so large, but an exception is made for art—unspoken acknowledgment, Tick suspects, that nobody considers art to be a real course, like history or math. Mrs. Roderigue isn't even full-time, teaching afternoons at the high school, mornings at the middle school, her teaching strategies identical regardless of her audience.

For Tick, the interesting thing about Mrs. Roderigue's color coding is that the tables themselves are all steel gray, so the only way to differentiate Blue from Red that first day was to read the signs—BLUE, GREEN, RED, YELLOW and BROWN, carefully lettered in black ink—taped to each. On the second day all the signs came down and were slipped into plastic baggies before they could be dirtied or wrinkled. Art, she told her students, was the study and practice of order. There was no such thing as Sloppy Art. Artists, she claimed, first had to know where they were, and in Mrs. Roderigue's class the first thing you learned was whether you were Blue or Green and so forth. If you were Blue, you were supposed to remember where Blue was, though *why* Blue was Blue, and not, for instance, a number, like "one" or "two," remained a mystery.

Nonetheless, at the Blue table, Tick sits next to Candace Burke, who favors trendy, girlie clothes—baggy jeans, tight shirts, pink Adidas shoes. Also, white eye shadow and lots of mascara. Today she's wearing her unicorn T-shirt. Either she's got two of these or she washes the one right after she's worn it. She'd worn it the first day of school and now, Thursday, she's wearing it again. "Oh-my-God-oh-my-God!" she exclaims, looking at Tick's painting. "You're almost done. I haven't even started. Help me, okay? What's my most vivid dream?"

"I don't know *any* of your dreams," Tick points out.

Candace shrugs, as if to suggest that that makes two of them, but this problem occupies her for no more than a split second. "So how come you're in here with the morons?" is what she'd really like to know. Though Candace has asked this every day, and been answered too, she either keeps forgetting or else is suspicious of the answers she's been given. Her persistence reminds Tick of a movie she saw once in which a man was interrogated for hours, asked all sorts of things, but one question, in particular, over and over. His answer was always the same, but his questioners must have suspected something, because they kept coming back to that one question. Finally, they killed him— out of frustration, apparently. You never found out whether the man was telling the truth or not.

Candace is openly using an Exacto knife she stole during the first day of class, carving the name of her boyfriend, Bobby, into the back of the wooden chair she's turned around and is sitting in the way older men sometimes do in the Empire Grill. Tick's proximity to this dangerous-looking instrument and the use to which it is being put are making her more than a little nervous, especially when Candace stops carving and gestures with the blade for dramatic emphasis. Tick half expects her to put the knife to her throat and hiss, "Why are you *really* in here with the morons? Who sent you? Tell me the truth or I'll—"

What Candace is trying to reconcile is that Tick is a high-track kid, whereas she herself and all the rest are "Bones," kids who take the lower-track versions of required courses like biology along with guaranteed GPA boosters like art. One reason Candace has befriended her, Tick suspects, is that she enjoys showing strangers around Bone

World, an academic sphere populated by those who can't learn grammar or solve math problems and see no reason why they should. The majority are boys, who don't at all mind being referred to as "Boners."

Candace herself prefers "moron." She confessed to Tick that it's also her mother's favorite word, one she applies to Candace on a wide variety of occasions, such as, "What's up, Moron?" or "You learn anything in school today, Moron?" or "Hey, Moron, you didn't walk off with my goddamn car keys again, did you?" or "I swear to fucking Christ, Moron, I catch you in the damn liquor cabinet again, I'm going to take you out of where you are and put you in Mount Calvary with the damn Christians, let you drink the Blood of the Lamb for a while and see how well you like that shit, and I can tell you right now you won't, so just stay *out* of my fucking vodka." As far as Tick can tell, Candace has concluded that the word is a term of endearment applied to kids like herself who happen, everyone seems to agree, to have no future.

Still, Tick wonders if she should voice her objection to the "moron" label before explaining why she happens to be among those thus classified. But since Candace doesn't appear to expect this, she decides not to. "I like art," Tick says weakly, just as she has every day this week, aware, as always, that the truth isn't much of a substitute for a good answer.

Tick almost didn't take art because it wouldn't fit into her schedule, being offered only at times when the high-track kids had required courses, like chemistry and calculus, or were at lunch. When Tick proposed that she could take art if she were allowed to eat lunch in the cafeteria during sixth period, the idea was vetoed until her father went with her to see the principal, Mr. Meyer, who pointed out that the cafeteria closed after fifth period. Even if Tick brought a sandwich with her and got a soda out of the machine, she'd have to eat it all by herself in the big, empty cafeteria, which would be locked after she entered, and she'd be on her honor not to let anyone else in, because there would be no monitor.

When Mr. Meyer asked Tick if she could live with these provisos, she wondered, as she so often did, at the strange world adults seemed to inhabit. Did they all suffer from some sort of collective amnesia? You had only to look at Mr. Meyer to know that he'd been the kind of fat kid everybody made fun of and that lunch had surely been a torment to him. He'd either gravitated naturally to the leper table or sat by himself at a table designed for sixteen, a target for all the kids overcrowding the cool tables, the tables that were identified as cool by who they were, and in Mrs. Roderigue's class the first thing you learned was whether you were Blue or Green and so forth. If you were Blue, you were supposed to remember where Blue was, though *why* Blue was Blue, and not, for instance, a number, like "one" or "two," remained a mystery.

Nonetheless, at the Blue table, Tick sits next to Candace Burke, who favors trendy, girlie clothes—baggy jeans, tight shirts, pink Adidas shoes. Also, white eye shadow and lots of mascara. Today she's wearing her unicorn T-shirt. Either she's got two of these or she washes the one right after she's worn it. She'd worn it the first day of school and now, Thursday, she's wearing it again. "Oh-my-God-oh-my-God!" she exclaims, looking at Tick's painting. "You're almost done. I haven't even started. Help me, okay? What's my most vivid dream?"

"I don't know *any* of your dreams," Tick points out.

Candace shrugs, as if to suggest that that makes two of them, but this problem occupies her for no more than a split second. "So how come you're in here with the morons?" is what she'd really like to know. Though Candace has asked this every day, and been answered too, she either keeps forgetting or else is suspicious of the answers she's been given. Her persistence reminds Tick of a movie she saw once in which a man was interrogated for hours, asked all sorts of things, but one question, in particular, over and over. His answer was always the same, but his questioners must have suspected something, because they kept coming back to that one question. Finally, they killed him— out of frustration, apparently. You never found out whether the man was telling the truth or not.

Candace is openly using an Exacto knife she stole during the first day of class, carving the name of her boyfriend, Bobby, into the back of the wooden chair she's turned around and is sitting in the way older men sometimes do in the Empire Grill. Tick's proximity to this dangerous-looking instrument and the use to which it is being put are making her more than a little nervous, especially when Candace stops carving and gestures with the blade for dramatic emphasis. Tick half expects her to put the knife to her throat and hiss, "Why are you *really* in here with the morons? Who sent you? Tell me the truth or I'll—"

What Candace is trying to reconcile is that Tick is a high-track kid, whereas she herself and all the rest are "Bones," kids who take the lower-track versions of required courses like biology along with guaranteed GPA boosters like art. One reason Candace has befriended her, Tick suspects, is that she enjoys showing strangers around Bone

World, an academic sphere populated by those who can't learn grammar or solve math problems and see no reason why they should. The majority are boys, who don't at all mind being referred to as "Boners."

Candace herself prefers "moron." She confessed to Tick that it's also her mother's favorite word, one she applies to Candace on a wide variety of occasions, such as, "What's up, Moron?" or "You learn anything in school today, Moron?" or "Hey, Moron, you didn't walk off with my goddamn car keys again, did you?" or "I swear to fucking Christ, Moron, I catch you in the damn liquor cabinet again, I'm going to take you out of where you are and put you in Mount Calvary with the damn Christians, let you drink the Blood of the Lamb for a while and see how well you like that shit, and I can tell you right now you won't, so just stay *out* of my fucking vodka." As far as Tick can tell, Candace has concluded that the word is a term of endearment applied to kids like herself who happen, everyone seems to agree, to have no future.

Still, Tick wonders if she should voice her objection to the "moron" label before explaining why she happens to be among those thus classified. But since Candace doesn't appear to expect this, she decides not to. "I like art," Tick says weakly, just as she has every day this week, aware, as always, that the truth isn't much of a substitute for a good answer.

Tick almost didn't take art because it wouldn't fit into her schedule, being offered only at times when the high-track kids had required courses, like chemistry and calculus, or were at lunch. When Tick proposed that she could take art if she were allowed to eat lunch in the cafeteria during sixth period, the idea was vetoed until her father went with her to see the principal, Mr. Meyer, who pointed out that the cafeteria closed after fifth period. Even if Tick brought a sandwich with her and got a soda out of the machine, she'd have to eat it all by herself in the big, empty cafeteria, which would be locked after she entered, and she'd be on her honor not to let anyone else in, because there would be no monitor.

When Mr. Meyer asked Tick if she could live with these provisos, she wondered, as she so often did, at the strange world adults seemed to inhabit. Did they all suffer from some sort of collective amnesia? You had only to look at Mr. Meyer to know that he'd been the kind of fat kid everybody made fun of and that lunch had surely been a torment to him. He'd either gravitated naturally to the leper table or sat by himself at a table designed for sixteen, a target for all the kids overcrowding the cool tables, the tables that were identified as cool by who had a right to sit at them, codes established the first day of school, the rules clear to everyone, no need for color-coding. You had only to look at Mr. Meyer to know he'd spent all his high school years getting hit in the back of the head with all manner of throwable food, yet here he was worried that Tick was going to miss out on the important "socialization" aspects of a good secondary education. Some damn thing must have hit him in the back of his pointed head pretty hard during one of those lunches, Tick decided, because the man honestly seemed to have no recollection of them.

Therefore, he had no idea how thrilled Tick was at the prospect of eating lunch by herself. She didn't mind in the least waiting until sixth period to eat her sandwich. School twisted her stomach into knots anyhow, and this way at least she wouldn't have to endure the humiliation of not having a place to sit. Which certainly would have been her destiny. She'd broken up with Zack Minty over the summer, meaning she would no longer be welcome at the table dominated by his circle. And she knew better than to try to crash one of the cliques at the popular girls' table. Far better to be alone in an empty cafeteria, Tick thought, than to be alone in a full one.

"Did you know Craig was going to buy me *The Beatles Anthology* for my birthday?" Candace wants to know now. "Before I broke up with him, I mean?"

Tick tries to ignore her. The first assignment is to paint your most vivid dream, and Tick's is the one where she's clutching a snake in her fist. The painting is going pretty well. The snake started out looking like an eel, but now it's less flat, more serpentine, except it's not as scary as the snake in her dream, which, no matter how tight her grip, manages to squirm up to where it can turn and look at her. In the dream she's safe as long as she can hold the snake up near its head, but each time it manages to slither through her grip. When it turns to look at her, she wakes up with a start. From this dream Tick concludes that she's learned something useful: whatever means you harm will look you over first.

"Are you listening to me?" Candace says.

"Who's Craig?" Tick asks, suspecting she's supposed to know, that he's somebody Candace has mentioned before, probably more than once. The good news is that Candace never minds repeating boyfriend stories.

"He's the one I broke up with for Bobby," she explains, preferring this subject to the task of beginning her thumbnail sketch, which she will later be required to transfer to a large piece of paper and then, finally, to paint. It doesn't appear to bother Candace that she's behind everybody in the class. More interesting, it doesn't seem to bother Mrs. Roderigue, either. All week long Tick has been expecting the woman to come around to the Blue table, see that Candace has done exactly nothing, and read her the riot act, but so far she's stayed strictly away, as if she's already determined that Blue is trouble and therefore doesn't exist.

Most teachers, Tick has learned, feel no great compulsion to confront trouble. They're never around when drugs are being bought and sold, for example. The mystery of the Exacto knife stolen after the first art class, its theft announced over the loudspeaker during homeroom, would be solved if Mrs. Roderigue ever visited Blue, where Candace openly uses it on her "Bobby" carving. Tick can't help but wonder if Mrs. Roderigue is as afraid of the knife as she is. Fear, often irrational, of the sort that paralyzes Tick, is something she'd like to think she'll outgrow. Adults, by and large, seem free of it. Even her Uncle David, whose car wreck nearly severed his arm at the elbow, seems almost carefree when he gets behind the wheel. No, most adults are more like her father, whose fear, if he feels any, has been replaced by a kind of melancholy. Her mother's a different story, though. Sometimes Tick sees a fleeting look of panic on Janine's face when she doesn't know she's being observed, but then she swallows hard and subdues whatever it is by sheer force of will. That's a trick Tick would be glad to learn, because dread is her more or less constant companion.

"So, should I wait for my boyfriend," Candace wants to know, "or go back with Craig for a couple weeks?"

Bobby, the one Candace may or may not wait for, is in jail. He was arrested at Fairhaven High, according to Candace, and it was not a righteous bust. Why she thinks this is not clear to Tick. Candace actually seems to believe the cops came for him because he took a dollar from his mother and only paid back seventy-five cents. Supposedly he'll be released in a couple weeks, in time for homecoming. Tick doesn't know how much of what Candace tells her is true. She's not sure, for instance, if the boy is really in jail. Or if he exists at all. Or if the other boy, Craig, ever really promised to buy her *The Beatles Anthology*. Vagaries of this sort make it hard to give good advice.

If she's to be believed, Candace has a very dramatic love life, which is fine with Tick, except that when she has finally exhausted the subject of her own romances she'll want to know about Tick's, which are sin-had a right to sit at them, codes established the first day of school, the rules clear to everyone, no need for color-coding. You had only to look at Mr. Meyer to know he'd spent all his high school years getting hit in the back of the head with all manner of throwable food, yet here he was worried that Tick was going to miss out on the important "socialization" aspects of a good secondary education. Some damn thing must have hit him in the back of his pointed head pretty hard during one of those lunches, Tick decided, because the man honestly seemed to have no recollection of them.

Therefore, he had no idea how thrilled Tick was at the prospect of eating lunch by herself. She didn't mind in the least waiting until sixth period to eat her sandwich. School twisted her stomach into knots anyhow, and this way at least she wouldn't have to endure the humiliation of not having a place to sit. Which certainly would have been her destiny. She'd broken up with Zack Minty over the summer, meaning she would no longer be welcome at the table dominated by his circle. And she knew better than to try to crash one of the cliques at the popular girls' table. Far better to be alone in an empty cafeteria, Tick thought, than to be alone in a full one.

"Did you know Craig was going to buy me *The Beatles Anthology* for my birthday?" Candace wants to know now. "Before I broke up with him, I mean?"

Tick tries to ignore her. The first assignment is to paint your most vivid dream, and Tick's is the one where she's clutching a snake in her fist. The painting is going pretty well. The snake started out looking like an eel, but now it's less flat, more serpentine, except it's not as scary as the snake in her dream, which, no matter how tight her grip, manages to squirm up to where it can turn and look at her. In the dream she's safe as long as she can hold the snake up near its head, but each time it manages to slither through her grip. When it turns to look at her, she wakes up with a start. From this dream Tick concludes that she's learned something useful: whatever means you harm will look you over first.

"Are you listening to me?" Candace says.

"Who's Craig?" Tick asks, suspecting she's supposed to know, that he's somebody Candace has mentioned before, probably more than once. The good news is that Candace never minds repeating boyfriend stories.

"He's the one I broke up with for Bobby," she explains, preferring this subject to the task of beginning her thumbnail sketch, which she will later be required to transfer to a large piece of paper and then, finally, to paint. It doesn't appear to bother Candace that she's behind everybody in the class. More interesting, it doesn't seem to bother Mrs. Roderigue, either. All week long Tick has been expecting the woman to come around to the Blue table, see that Candace has done exactly nothing, and read her the riot act, but so far she's stayed strictly away, as if she's already determined that Blue is trouble and therefore doesn't exist.

Most teachers, Tick has learned, feel no great compulsion to confront trouble. They're never around when drugs are being bought and sold, for example. The mystery of the Exacto knife stolen after the first art class, its theft announced over the loudspeaker during homeroom, would be solved if Mrs. Roderigue ever visited Blue, where Candace openly uses it on her "Bobby" carving. Tick can't help but wonder if Mrs. Roderigue is as afraid of the knife as she is. Fear, often irrational, of the sort that paralyzes Tick, is something she'd like to think she'll outgrow. Adults, by and large, seem free of it. Even her Uncle David, whose car wreck nearly severed his arm at the elbow, seems almost carefree when he gets behind the wheel. No, most adults are more like her father, whose fear, if he feels any, has been replaced by a kind of melancholy. Her mother's a different story, though. Sometimes Tick sees a fleeting look of panic on Janine's face when she doesn't know she's being observed, but then she swallows hard and subdues whatever it is by sheer force of will. That's a trick Tick would be glad to learn, because dread is her more or less constant companion.

"So, should I wait for my boyfriend," Candace wants to know, "or go back with Craig for a couple weeks?"

Bobby, the one Candace may or may not wait for, is in jail. He was arrested at Fairhaven High, according to Candace, and it was not a righteous bust. Why she thinks this is not clear to Tick. Candace actually seems to believe the cops came for him because he took a dollar from his mother and only paid back seventy-five cents. Supposedly he'll be released in a couple weeks, in time for homecoming. Tick doesn't know how much of what Candace tells her is true. She's not sure, for instance, if the boy is really in jail. Or if he exists at all. Or if the other boy, Craig, ever really promised to buy her *The Beatles Anthology*. Vagaries of this sort make it hard to give good advice.

If she's to be believed, Candace has a very dramatic love life, which is fine with Tick, except that when she has finally exhausted the subject of her own romances she'll want to know about Tick's, which are singularly lacking in drama. Or maybe just singularly lacking. On Martha's Vineyard she'd met a shy boy from Indiana who was visiting friends with his mother while her divorce from the boy's father became final; if Tick were to steal an Exacto knife and carve a boy's name in the back of her chair, the name would be "Donny." When he told her about his father, who was moving to California, his eyes filled with tears. His father was moving right then, that very week, and Donny had been packed off to Martha's Vineyard, he'd confided, so he wouldn't have to watch him leave home. Donny also told her he'd have preferred to live with his dad, even though he was the one at fault, for falling in love with another woman.

Tick told him that this had been pretty much her experience, too; after her parents split up, nobody had asked her who she wanted to live with. Of course, in her case nobody was moving to California, and although she technically was living with her mother, she spent almost as much time with her father. Donny found it hard to believe that Tick's mother and father still lived about three blocks from each other; his father, apparently, had selected San Diego as his new home because it was as far from Indianapolis as you could get without leaving the continental United States. Tick explained that her parents probably just didn't have enough money to put much distance between themselves.

This intimate conversation had taken place on the beach on their last night together, and Donny had taken her hand as they watched the orange sun plunge into the ocean. They hadn't even found the courage to kiss, and early the next morning when they'd said their good-byes, they'd shaken hands there in front of Tick's father and Donny's mother, unsure that anything more would be allowed them, their fingers icy-cold with disappointment.

Anyway, it wasn't much of a story to tell someone like Candace, even if Tick was inclined to share it. She suspects it's mostly evidence of her own stunted emotional and romantic development, as is the fact that she can't seem to stop thinking about how good it was to sit there on the warm sand in the gathering dusk and just hold hands with a boy she liked. Sure, she wishes now that they'd found the courage to kiss, but at the time they'd both been content. Their mutual understanding, even though it was an understanding of grief, had at first been thrilling, then quietly reassuring, though she doubts Candace would see it that way. She's already made several references to going down on Bobby. Tick is almost sure she knows what going down on a boy means, and if she's right, Candace won't be impressed by an encounter that climaxed with hand-holding.

"I mean, Craig's not so bad, and he loves me and everything . . . and he really wants to buy me *The Beatles Anthology*, so, like, what should I do?" Candace wants to know.

Before Tick can say anything, they're interrupted by a boy named Justin who's sitting at the far end of their table.

"What, Candace?" he says, pretending she'd spoken to him. "You say you want to make out with John?"

John Voss, also at the Blue table, never even looks up. Of all the kids at Empire High, he seems to Tick the most unknowable, and for this reason he scares her a little. It isn't so much his strange, thrift-shop clothes or his hair cut in patches, as if he'd done the job himself. It's his silence. So far this week, he hasn't spoken a word. Were he not referred to every now and then by Justin, who pretends to narrate the comatose boy's thoughts, everyone would forget he is even there. John Voss is painting something elaborately filigreed in the shape of an egg, which is also confusing and frightening Tick. Who dreams of eggs? Watching him work makes Tick think of analogies of the sort she encounters on standardized tests. This one would read: *John is to Justin as* BLANK *is to Candace.* The answer would be *Tick*.

"John says you should come over to his house today after school, Candace. He says he's got something he'd like to show you."

"Shut up, you asshole!" Candace shouts, startling Tick. The panic in her voice results, Tick knows, from Justin's attempt to link her romantically with this boy who is at the very bottom of the high school's social hierarchy. Since Candace isn't so far from the bottom herself, she must guard against any misunderstanding of this sort. "I'm sorry, Mrs. Roderigue," she says when everyone from Red, Green, Yellow and Brown turns to look at her, "but Justin is always embarrassing me."

Mrs. Roderigue has indeed straightened up and is now glaring at Blue, as if everyone at the table were equally responsible for Candace's outburst. Her disappointment and displeasure seem to include, for instance, Tick herself and John Voss, who still hasn't even looked up from his egg. "I hope," the teacher intones, "that we will have no more outbursts from the Blue table."

"I *said* I'm sorry," Candace responds audibly, rolling her eyes as if to suggest that it's hard for her to imagine what the woman could possibly want from her that she hasn't already given.

"If you require a model for acceptable behavior," Mrs. Roderigue continues, as if she imagines that this might truly be the problem, "you need look no further than Green."

The Green table, Tick notes, is decimated by absenteeism today. Normally it has eight students, but four are missing; two of those present are reading their algebra books in preparation for a test next period, and another is fast asleep with his head on the table. If she didn't know better, Tick would like to raise her hand and ask Mrs. Roderigue precisely what it is about the Green table that's so worthy of emulation. Even Candace, using a stolen Exacto knife to carve her jailed boyfriend's name in ornate letters, memorializing her affection for a juvenile delinquent and thereby defacing school property, comes closer to fulfilling the implied objectives of an art course.

"So, how come you broke up with Zack Minty?" Candace asks, once Mrs. Roderigue has returned her attention to the creative efforts of the favored Red table.

"We kind of broke up with each other," Tick says, which is true in a way. When she'd told Zack she didn't want to go out with him anymore, he'd said fine, that he didn't want to go out with her anymore either. Like, who did she think she was, anyway? He'd called the next day to tell her he already had a new girlfriend, naming a girl who seemed to hate Tick, despite their never having exchanged a word.

"I think you should get back together with him," Candace says, apparently uninhibited by knowing virtually nothing about the relationship. "I mean, he still really loves you."

Tick swallows hard, tries to concentrate on her snake, which suddenly feels wrong in some way she can't exactly put her finger on. True, it *is* looking less like an eel, which is good, but there's something definitely wrong about its proportions, as if the lower part of its body were drawn to one scale and the upper, including its head, to another. She wishes she could justify this as perspective. A lot of bad art, it seems to her, gets excused as intentional.

"I doubt it," Tick says, resorting to the absolute, unadorned truth this time.

The odd thing was that before she went to the Vineyard, she hadn't known what to do about Zack. Summer was one thing, but it was much harder to be friendless during the school year when as a friendless person you were constantly on display. Losing Zack wasn't so bad in itself. At least she didn't have to wonder every day what kind of mood he was in, whether he'd be nice or mean, his behavior about as predictable as the wind. So being without a boyfriend was okay, even though she doubted she'd find another anytime soon. What worried her more than losing Zack was losing his friends, the whole Zack network. While they were together, *his* friends had been *her* friends, but as soon as they broke up, she discovered the truth: that they were *his* friends, every one of them. Not that they disliked her. She suspected that a couple of them actually liked her better than they liked Zack, or would've been happy to remain neutral, had the rules permitted any such thing. But they didn't, and Zack wasn't someone you wanted for an enemy. Right away she'd started getting calls from his friends urging her to get back together with him, hinting that she wouldn't be welcome in their group otherwise. A couple of the boys sounded almost afraid, like they couldn't imagine the kind of recklessness she was contemplating. One of the girls even volunteered that Zack might be willing to break up with this new girlfriend if Tick came back, maybe, though it wasn't for sure.

Until Martha's Vineyard she'd seriously considered doing so, but now she was pretty sure she couldn't. After being with a boy who actually liked her, she was willing to be friendless, at least for now. What saddened her was the cost of this new knowledge. Could it be that getting the taste of affection, so sweet and new, from somebody who wasn't your father or mother, meant that she'd have to forgo other companionship entirely?

"I mean, he totally does *not* care about Heather," Candace is saying. "You should, like, see the way he treats her."

"I know how he treats her," Tick says, studying her snake critically. What it needs, she decides, is a tongue. "It's how he used to treat me."

"He's changed," Candace says, looking at her now. She's stopped carving entirely and is gathering up her things in anticipation of the bell. Her sudden interest in Tick's romantic life confirms what Tick has been fearing: that Candace is befriending her because she was specifically commissioned by Zack to sound her out on the subject of a possible reconciliation. Tick has seen blessedly little of him since school began, but that's because of football practice, which he has to attend every day after classes. If it weren't for that, he would have been tormenting her nonstop. The other thing saving her is that Zack screwed up so badly last year that he was booted out of the high-track courses. Otherwise he'd be sitting right behind her in chemistry and

American lit, and she'd be feeling the weight of his wounded, angry eyes all day long.

Now that Tick is sure about Candace's motives it angers her, and before she can consider the wisdom of doing so, she says, "I've changed, too. The biggest change is that I don't like him anymore."

Candace's response to this is to let loose the loudest scream Tick has ever heard. John Voss, at the other end of the table, actually looks up from his egg. Something metallic rattles onto the floor next to Tick's clog, and Candace, howling oh-my-God-oh-my-God, holds up her hand, which is gushing blood from a deep gash that extends from her thumbnail almost to her palm. The blood is everywhere— down her arm, in the elaborate grooves she's been carving in the back of her chair, even a small pink drop on Tick's snake. Looking at all the blood, Tick feels her own left arm begin to throb the way it always does in anticipation of hypodermic needles at the doctor's office, and at horror movies when somebody gets slashed.

Candace, still screaming, wraps her thumb in the palm of her other hand and bends rapidly back and forth at the waist like one of those mechanical birds sipping water at an imaginary pool. There's blood down the front of her unicorn shirt now, and the cowards at the Green table have all gotten up and moved away to the back wall.

Tick's left arm now hurts so bad that she's beginning to feel light-headed, and the whole room takes on an odd sheen, blurred at the edges like a television dream sequence. She leans forward, resting her forehead on the cool metal table and listening to Candace shriek until another voice, sounding far off, joins in and a new pair of feet appear next to Candace's. Tick identifies them as Mrs. Roderigue's, and way off she hears the woman shouting, "Take your hand away so I can see, child." And then, "Who did this to you?"

Now Candace is screaming, "I'm-sorry-oh-my-God-I'm-so-sorry." Tick, confused, concludes that Candace must be talking to her, apologizing for acting as Zack Minty's go-between. "It's okay," Tick says, or imagines saying, probably, since she's unable to lift her head from the table to speak. In any case, it's what she would like to say, because she's the kind of person who forgives easily, who in fact cannot bear to think of a person wanting to be forgiven and having that forgiveness withheld, and so the words "it's okay," spoken or unspoken, ring in her ears along with the rush of her own blood. When it seems the pain in her left arm can't get any worse without the arm itself exploding, the pain peaks and then everything gradually becomes vague. Tick, now sweating and shivering, fears that for things to right themselves again, she'll have to cross back through that territory of pain, and the truth is she'd rather not. She'd rather pass out.

Only when she opens her eyes does she realize she's been clenching them tightly shut for some time. With her forehead still on the cool edge of the table, she has a view of the floor at her feet. There, between her right foot and her backpack, is the bloody Exacto knife. Candace's screaming has stopped, and there's no sign of her pink Adidases. Mrs. Roderigue, who seems to have gone away somewhere and come back again, is urging Tick to raise her head, and this time she discovers that she can. She's even more surprised to see that the room has emptied and that all the kids are clustered out in the hall, peering in at her. According to the clock on the wall, ten minutes have passed. Mrs. Roderigue is running her thumb along the metal edge of Candace's chair, apparently trying to locate a surface sharp enough to slice a kid's thumb open to the bone. The principal, Mr. Meyer, elbows his way into the room, then comes over and puts his hand on Tick's forehead.

"I wouldn't get too close," Mrs. Roderigue says. "She looks like she might puke."

Mr. Meyer reacts visibly to this intelligence, though Tick can't tell for sure whether he's startled by that possibility or by his teacher's crudeness.

"I think I'm okay," Tick says, in case it's the former that's worrying her principal. "What happened?"

"You fainted, angel," Mr. Meyer said, making her like him for the very first time. "The sight of all that—"

He breaks off his thought, worried perhaps that the word "blood" might have the same effect as the sight of blood. "You want me to call your mom and dad?" He catches himself as soon as he says this, probably remembering that her parents are separated.

Tick, wiggling the fingers of her left hand, repeats that she thinks she's going to be all right. The fingers now feel like they're being poked by a thousand needles, but otherwise there's no pain, which means she's going to come out of this in a new place, which is a relief, not having to enter that same dark tunnel of pain again.

After instructing her to remain where she is, Mr. Meyer takes Mrs. Roderigue aside. Tick is still able to overhear small snatches of their conversation, Mrs. Roderigue explaining how Candace told her she'd sliced her thumb open. Now it's Mr. Meyer's turn to examine the back of the chair, turning it upside down, running his own thumb along the metal surfaces tentatively, as if he isn't sure whether he really wants to solve this mystery or not. Tick reaches under the table, as if for her backpack, picks up the Exacto knife, and slips it into one of the open side pouches.

When she straightens up, shouldering her backpack, Mr. Meyer takes her gently by the elbow and guides her toward the door. There she catches a glimpse of Zack Minty out in the corridor and a wave of nausea passes over her quickly, her knees wobbly for a second, and Mr. Meyer catches her around the waist. Normally Tick hates being touched, especially by adults, but this time she's grateful.

"The nurse's room for you, young lady," Mr. Meyer says, steering her in the right direction. It occurs to Tick then that she and Candace have sink duty this week and they haven't done their cleanup, which Mrs. Roderigue has made clear is the most important part of the whole artistic process. When she glances back into the room, she sees Mrs. Roderigue standing at the Blue table, as if to suggest that it's safe to visit Blue now that its artists are all gone. She's looking at Tick's snake with an expression of extreme distaste.

CHAPTER 5

THE DONUT SHOP in Empire Falls had always been one of Max Roby's favorite places because of its smoking policy, which was, "Go ahead. See if we care." Miles wondered what his father was going to do next year when all Maine restaurants would by law become smoke-free. For the present there was still a cigarette machine by the door, and with only eight booths and a counter with half a dozen stools there could be no nonsmoking section, which pleased the old man even more than being allowed to light up. Max was the kind of guy who created his own atmosphere, and he took particular pleasure, it seemed to Miles, in knowing that other people had to breathe his air when he was done with it. Actually, smoking was only one manifestation of this phenomenon. Max had always enjoyed breaking his own containment. He liked to stand close to people when he talked; and when he was eating, food had a way of becoming airborne. Now, at seventy, he'd developed a sweet tooth. He would've eaten chocolate bars if his teeth had allowed it, but half of them were gone and the other half loose, so he settled for sugar donuts. By the time Max was finished with one, Miles, who usually just drank coffee, often found his entire shirtfront dusted with confectioners' sugar.

Many years ago, Miles had asked his mother what had attracted her to a man with such disgusting personal habits, and she'd replied that his father hadn't always been this way, certainly not as a young man. Miles loved his mother and would've liked to believe her, but it wasn't easy. All her life she'd been a woman who, once she gave her heart, would ignore anything dismaying, but Miles suspected she'd learned to overlook Max entirely in order to stay married to him. Still, by the time Miles asked, she was clearly mortified by her choice of a mate. "You'd never guess it to look at him now," she told her son, "but your father had the most infectious smile."

Infectious Miles could believe. Like most kids, when Miles and his brother were growing up, they brought a great variety of illnesses home from school—chicken pox, mumps, measles, routine colds and flus. David proved particularly susceptible to whatever was going around, and stayed sick longer than Miles did, but neither boy could be described as sickly, except when their father brought something home and shared it with them. Then everyone but Max himself went down for the mandatory eight count. Whatever the virus, it became several degrees more deadly in his pulmonary system until he finally reintroduced it into the atmosphere by means of his explosive sneezes. Max regarded covering his mouth as irrational behavior. The way he looked at it, you might as well cover your ass with your hand when you farted. See how much good that did.

Miles watched his father light a fresh cigarette with his old one before crushing out the butt in the ashtray he'd managed to half fill in twenty minutes. Miles studied his father's mouth, trying to imagine a full set of white teeth and that infectious grin, but it was no use. One of the great unsolved mysteries of the universe, Miles had long believed, was what women found attractive about certain men. Apparently women all over the world wanted to have sex with Mick Jagger, or at least had wanted to once upon a time. Others had not found Max Roby repulsive. Miles couldn't help admiring women for their ability to dismiss the evidence of their senses. If that's what explained it. If it wasn't simply that from time to time they were unaccountably drawn to the grotesque.

Outside, it was drizzling again, as it had the day before, just hard enough to make painting impossible. Half an hour earlier, Miles, heading back to the restaurant, had seen his father sitting on one of the benches outside the Empire Towers, talking to an old woman who seemed to be wondering what she'd done to deserve his company and how she might avoid making the same mistake in the future. "Just keep driving," Miles had said out loud, even as he pulled the Jetta over and tooted the horn. No good deed, he reminded himself as Max hopped up from the bench and came toward him across the newly seeded lawn, goes unpunished.

Nor would this one, Miles added to himself, studying his father across the booth. "You've got crumbs in your beard, Dad," he pointed out. "Did you know that?" Max shaved only every third or fourth day, and he never ironed the clothes he abandoned in the communal dryers of the Towers complex until one of the other residents removed and returned them. The result was a web of crazy pleats and wrinkles in everything he wore.

"So what?" the old man wanted to know, drawing in another lungful of smoke, then expelling it off to the side in deference to Miles, who didn't smoke. As if the air weren't blue all around them. As if Miles and David hadn't smoked the equivalent of a pack a day since they were babies whenever their father was around.

"You look like an idiot is what," Miles told him. "People are going to take one look at you and conclude you're as senile as Father Tom." Actually, next to Max, Father Tom looked positively elegant.

Max appeared to consider this possibility for a full beat before dismissing it. "You should let me help you out with the church," he said, reminded of this desire by Miles's reference to the old priest. Painting the church was a subject Miles considered closed and Max considered wide-open. "I did paint houses for forty years, you know. I'm supposed to go down to the Keys in another month. How do you expect me to do that if I don't have any money?"

"I don't think helping me paint is a good idea, Dad," Miles said. "Last month you fell off a barstool. I don't want you falling off any ladders."

"That's different," his father explained. "I was drunk."

"Right," Miles said. "As I'm sure you'll be when you fall off the ladder."

His father nodded agreeably, and if Miles hadn't known better he'd have sworn Max had given in.

But when the old man exhaled this time, he didn't turn his head.

"If I had a few bucks in my pocket, I wouldn't have to hit you up all the time, you know."

The waitress appeared, refilled their coffee cups, and departed again in one fluid motion, suggesting to Miles that she was dead set against lingering in Max Roby's proximity.

"Did you hear what I said?" his father wanted to know.

"I heard you, Dad," Miles answered, emptying a packet of sweetener into his coffee. "But you keep forgetting that I'm painting St. Cat's for free."

His father shrugged. "That doesn't mean *you* can't pay me."

"Yes, it does, Dad," Miles said. "That's precisely what it means."

The last thing Miles wanted was Max working alongside him at the church. Every time Max saw Father Mark, he'd rag him about how cheap Catholics were; he reasoned that since the Vatican was rich, all priests, by virtue of being employed by the Vatican, could write checks at will. How could the church have all those millions stashed away and not be able to afford to pay two poor house painters in Empire Falls, Maine? That's what he'd want Father Mark to explain. Actually, the question would be rhetorical, since Max would allow Father Mark about two seconds before explaining how the church operated this scam. Every week, he'd argue, you collect money from people who don't know any better than to give it to you, then you put it in a bank halfway around the world where nobody from Empire Falls, Maine, is likely to look for it, much less find it. If anybody ever asks you for part of it back—say, to have your own damn church painted—you tell them the money's all gone, that you're as poor as they are, that you gave the money in question to the bishop, who gave it to the cardinal, who gave it to the pope. "In my next life," Max would conclude, "that's who I want to be. The pope. And I'll do the same thing he does. I'll keep all the goddamn money." Miles enjoyed scripting scenes like this, mostly because doing so helped him to avoid them in reality.

"If you paid me for work," continued Max, whose rhetoric was more sophisticated than you might expect from a man with food in his beard, "I wouldn't have to feel worthless. There's no law says old people have to feel worthless all the while, you know. You paid me, I'd have some dignity."

Now it was Miles's turn to nod and smile agreeably. "I think the dignity ship set sail a long time ago, Dad."

Max grinned, then finished stirring his coffee and used his spoon to point at his son, who felt a couple stray drops of coffee fleck his shirt-front. "You're trying to hurt my feelings," his father said knowingly, "but you can't."

Miles dabbed a wet paper napkin on the spots. "Besides, Dad," he said, "anytime you feel like an infusion of dignity, you can come down to the restaurant and wash dishes for a while."

"That's your idea of dignity? Coop your old man up in that little room with no windows for hours, washing dishes for minimum wage? Half of which goes to the government?"

Which Max would do, eventually, when he got needy enough. Miles was in no hurry to have him give in, either, since the old man was a careless, resentful worker. In his opinion any dish that came out of the Hobart was clean by definition, no matter if it was stained yellow with egg yolk. He hated, even more than the claustrophobic room, Miles's refusal to pay him under the table. He reckoned that if you could paint a whole house under the table—and he had, all his working life—then you ought to be able to wash a few dishes under there too. In Max's view, Grace had raised their son to be morally fastidious just to spite him. Had he foreseen such moral inflexibility, he'd have taken more of a personal interest in the boy's education, but unfortunately he hadn't noticed until it was too late. His other son, David, had more give to him, thank God.

"I'd let you hire me at the restaurant if I could come out and work the counter now and then," Max said. "There's nothing to flipping a burger, you know. And I like talking to people."

"I'd have to run you through the Hobart first," Miles told him. "Rinse some of the crumbs out of your beard. You don't seem to understand that people come into the Empire Grill to eat, and you're a walking appetite suppressant."

"I may be sempty," his father continued without missing a beat, "but I can still climb like a monkey."

Back to painting the church again. The old man *was* nimble, Miles had to admit, both of foot and of conversation. Miles had given up trying to corner him long ago.

Max's persistence about the church was curious, though. Thirty years ago, when Father Tom had hired another contractor to paint St. Catherine's, his father had vowed never to set foot on the grounds again. Of course he hadn't set foot inside for a decade anyway, leaving his wife and son (David wasn't yet born) to attend services. The way Max saw it, though, was that everything his wife and son did, they did under his aegis, and the contractor Father Tom had hired was a damn Presbyterian, not even remotely connected to the parish. Maybe Max wasn't a practicing Catholic himself, but he was married to one who practiced every minute of her life, even though she had it all down pat. Also, he'd bred another little Catholic, and that should have counted, too.

Still, Max had been true to his pledge, which now caused Miles to wonder. Was his desire to help paint the church some kind of oblique regret? Miles had never known his father to indulge regret in any form, though he'd had more than his fair share of opportunities. After all, Max had made a poor effort at being a father and an even poorer one at being a husband. In truth he wasn't even much of a house painter. He didn't like to scrape, and he laid the paint on thick and sloppy. He preferred sitting in bars to painting houses, and so, to proceed from the former to the latter, he liked to work fast, even in circumstances that cried out for deliberation. He painted windows shut and couldn't be bothered to wipe the glass off with a rag if he'd managed to swipe it with a brush.

In any other man his age a desire to paint the church might have represented nothing more than a longing to spend some time with his neglected son, but Miles doubted this was the case with Max, who'd never given much evidence of enjoying the company of either of his sons, though he did appreciate anyone who'd spring for a donut so he could put the price of the donut toward a pack of cigarettes. No, the only conclusion that Miles could come to was that old age generally played havoc with your personality. Father Tom, for instance, who had always assigned the hearing of confessions to the junior priests, now, in his dotage, pleaded with Father Mark to let him hear just a few. If the younger priest wasn't vigilant on Saturday afternoons, he'd look up and find the old priest had disappeared and then would have to hurry across the lawn between the rectory and the church to the dark confessional, where the old man would be patiently awaiting further revelations from his parishioners, curious now, in his old age, about what people were up to, and eager to share what he'd learned. It was from Father Tom that Miles first learned his wife was carrying on with Walt Comeau.

"I'll tell you another thing, too. Once I'm up on a ladder, I don't get scared like some little girl."

"Works both ways, Dad," Miles reminded him. "You can't hurt my feelings either."

"Never meant to," the old man said, exhibiting a kind of straightforward insincerity that was, in its own way, endearing. "When did you become such a damn sissy about heights, is what I'd like to know? I'm sempty and I can still climb like a monkey. And you're what?"

"Forty-two."

"Forty-two." Max stubbed out his cigarette, as if at least the question of his son's age had been established beyond question. "Forty-two and afraid to climb a stepladder. I fell two damn stories once and *I'm* not scared."

"Finish your coffee, Dad," Miles said. "I need to get back to the restaurant."

"I fell off a scaffold over on Division Street—two damn stories— and landed on my ass in the middle of a rosebush. Try that sometime. That don't mean I'm afraid to climb a ladder anymore."

Outside, a police cruiser pulled into the parking lot, and Miles saw it was Jimmy Minty at the wheel. He could feel the cruiser's front bumper actually nudge the side of the building, causing the Formica booth, as well as its ashtrays, to shudder. Instead of getting out, Jimmy—in uniform today—just sat there, his lips moving as if in conversation with an invisible companion. Only when he leaned forward to hang up the receiver did it dawn on Miles that he'd been talking into his radio. This made three times in two days that their paths had crossed. Coincidentally. Well, it *was* possible.

"I could help you rig the platforms at least," his father was saying. "That way you'd know you were standing on something solid."

"I know how to rig scaffolding, Dad."

"I should hope so," Max said. "I'm the one taught you how, in case you forgot."

"I didn't forget."

"I let *you* help, if you recall. If your mother'd known she'd have had a fit, but I let you help anyway. Now I need some traveling expenses and you tell me to take a hike."

"I never said—"

"I gotta pee," his father said disgustedly, sliding out of the booth, as if the conversation, not the coffee, had caused this unfortunate need to relieve himself.

The restroom door had no sooner closed behind Max than Jimmy Minty slipped into the booth, setting his shiny black hat on the table. His red hair was going a little gray at the temples, Miles noticed.

The waitress set a cup of coffee in front of him. "I wish you wouldn't run into that wall every time you pull in, Jimmy," she said. "You scare the hell out of people. One minute they're drinking coffee and minding their own business, and the next minute you're parkin' in the booth with them. It's not like the side of this damn building's invisible. The idea is to stop before you get to it."

"You need to get a couple of those concrete curbs out there." Minty smiled. "I bet I'm not the only one who taps that wall, Shirley."

regret? Miles had never known his father to indulge regret in any form, though he'd had more than his fair share of opportunities. After all, Max had made a poor effort at being a father and an even poorer one at being a husband. In truth he wasn't even much of a house painter. He didn't like to scrape, and he laid the paint on thick and sloppy. He preferred sitting in bars to painting houses, and so, to proceed from the former to the latter, he liked to work fast, even in circumstances that cried out for deliberation. He painted windows shut and couldn't be bothered to wipe the glass off with a rag if he'd managed to swipe it with a brush.

In any other man his age a desire to paint the church might have represented nothing more than a longing to spend some time with his neglected son, but Miles doubted this was the case with Max, who'd never given much evidence of enjoying the company of either of his sons, though he did appreciate anyone who'd spring for a donut so he could put the price of the donut toward a pack of cigarettes. No, the only conclusion that Miles could come to was that old age generally played havoc with your personality. Father Tom, for instance, who had always assigned the hearing of confessions to the junior priests, now, in his dotage, pleaded with Father Mark to let him hear just a few. If the younger priest wasn't vigilant on Saturday afternoons, he'd look up and find the old priest had disappeared and then would have to hurry across the lawn between the rectory and the church to the dark confessional, where the old man would be patiently awaiting further revelations from his parishioners, curious now, in his old age, about what people were up to, and eager to share what he'd learned. It was from Father Tom that Miles first learned his wife was carrying on with Walt Comeau.

"I'll tell you another thing, too. Once I'm up on a ladder, I don't get scared like some little girl."

"Works both ways, Dad," Miles reminded him. "You can't hurt my feelings either."

"Never meant to," the old man said, exhibiting a kind of straightforward insincerity that was, in its own way, endearing. "When did you become such a damn sissy about heights, is what I'd like to know? I'm sempty and I can still climb like a monkey. And you're what?"

"Forty-two."

"Forty-two." Max stubbed out his cigarette, as if at least the question of his son's age had been established beyond question. "Forty-two and afraid to climb a stepladder. I fell two damn stories once and *I'm* not scared."

"Finish your coffee, Dad," Miles said. "I need to get back to the restaurant."

"I fell off a scaffold over on Division Street—two damn stories— and landed on my ass in the middle of a rosebush. Try that sometime. That don't mean I'm afraid to climb a ladder anymore."

Outside, a police cruiser pulled into the parking lot, and Miles saw it was Jimmy Minty at the wheel. He could feel the cruiser's front bumper actually nudge the side of the building, causing the Formica booth, as well as its ashtrays, to shudder. Instead of getting out, Jimmy—in uniform today—just sat there, his lips moving as if in conversation with an invisible companion. Only when he leaned forward to hang up the receiver did it dawn on Miles that he'd been talking into his radio. This made three times in two days that their paths had crossed. Coincidentally. Well, it *was* possible.

"I could help you rig the platforms at least," his father was saying. "That way you'd know you were standing on something solid."

"I know how to rig scaffolding, Dad."

"I should hope so," Max said. "I'm the one taught you how, in case you forgot."

"I didn't forget."

"I let *you* help, if you recall. If your mother'd known she'd have had a fit, but I let you help anyway. Now I need some traveling expenses and you tell me to take a hike."

"I never said—"

"I gotta pee," his father said disgustedly, sliding out of the booth, as if the conversation, not the coffee, had caused this unfortunate need to relieve himself.

The restroom door had no sooner closed behind Max than Jimmy Minty slipped into the booth, setting his shiny black hat on the table. His red hair was going a little gray at the temples, Miles noticed.

The waitress set a cup of coffee in front of him. "I wish you wouldn't run into that wall every time you pull in, Jimmy," she said. "You scare the hell out of people. One minute they're drinking coffee and minding their own business, and the next minute you're parkin' in the booth with them. It's not like the side of this damn building's invisible. The idea is to stop before you get to it."

"You need to get a couple of those concrete curbs out there." Minty smiled. "I bet I'm not the only one who taps that wall, Shirley."

"No," she admitted. "You're just the only one who hits it every time."

When she stepped away, the policeman shrugged. "Hey, Miles. I thought that was your Jetta out there. You should've spent the extra for the undercoating. What would it have run you—couple hundred?"

It never took Jimmy Minty long to turn any conversation to one about money. He particularly liked to draw Miles's attention to whatever was wrong with any of his possessions, such as rust on the Jetta, of which there was plenty. Miles had long suspected that Jimmy Minty considered him some kind of yardstick by which he might measure his own economic well-being. The oddest thing about this, Miles thought, was that it seemed a direct extension of their childhoods on Long Street. Jimmy Minty had always taken careful inventory of Miles's belongings, wanting to know how much everything cost and where it was purchased. If they got similar Christmas presents, Jimmy liked to explain why his was better, that it had been purchased smarter and cheaper because *his* dad knew where to go—even if the toy in question was obviously a cheap knockoff. After detailing the advantages of his present, he'd suggest they switch, just for a while; often, before Jimmy returned it, Miles's toy would get broken.

Even thirty years later Miles could still remember the relief he felt when his mother took him out of the public grade school and enrolled him at Sacred Heart, where Jimmy—the family was not Catholic— could not follow. Gradually, though they remained neighbors, the boys' lives began to drift apart, and by the time they were thrown together again in high school, they had different lives, different friends. Of course, Jimmy's, as he explained to Miles, were better. After graduation he did a stint in the service while Miles was away at college, and by the time Miles returned to Empire Falls, Jimmy was newly married and living in Fairhaven. He visited his parents, though, and after Miles and Janine got married he made overtures about striking up their old friendship, something Miles didn't particularly desire, since the grown-up Jimmy Minty had the same way of taking inventory behind his eyes, only now he was comparing wives. For the last decade, they had seldom seen each other, except in moving vehicles or when Jimmy had a new toy he wanted to show off in the Empire Grill. The last time—a year ago—he'd ordered a steak and then lingered at the counter drinking coffee until Miles deigned to notice the red Camaro parked out front. On any such occasion Jimmy would assure Miles that he was doing all right for himself, despite having been denied opportunities like college. If he kept his nose clean, he didn't see any reason he shouldn't be the next chief of police of Empire Falls. His son, Zack, though—*he* was going to have it made.

"That your dad I saw with you?" Jimmy wondered now, nodding toward the men's room.

"You know it was. You sat right there"— Miles nodded through the window at the cruiser—"staring at us."

"The light was reflecting off the glass," Minty said. "It could've been anybody."

"Hell of a guess, then."

"Sorry about yesterday," he said, apparently in reference to the young police officer who had interrogated Miles on Long Street. "New kid. Still learning the ropes. Good thing I happened by, though. You talk back to him or something?"

"Not even remotely."

Minty shrugged. "Well, you pissed him off somehow. Good thing I turned up when I did."

This second reference to his good fortune, Miles realized, was intended as another chance for Miles to express his gratitude. That he should fail to take advantage of it was visibly disappointing, but Jimmy seemed determined to get over it.

"Breaks your heart, doesn't it?" he said. "The old neighborhood?"

Miles tried to navigate their talk into the calmer waters of generality. "The whole town, for that matter."

Jimmy Minty's surprised, even hurt expression suggested that he considered this indictment of Empire Falls far too sweeping. "I still like it here," he said. "I can't help it, I just do. People say there are better places, but I don't know." He paused in case Miles wanted to rattle off a list of supposedly better places. "Long Street, though. That's different. I get called up there all the time these days. Nothing but wife beaters and drug dealers anymore."

"Wife beaters aren't anything new," Miles reminded him, since Jimmy's own father, William, had been known to settle marital differences in this fashion.

Jimmy ignored him. "Hell, the place you were parked out front of is the biggest drug house in town." He lowered his voice now. "We've been monitoring who goes in and out for a while. I guess Officer Pollard thought you were there to make a score."

Miles couldn't help smiling. "Somebody should tell him he'll have better luck, evidence-wise, if he waits until suspects come out, instead of busting them on the way in."

"That's what I told him. You gotta admit, though, that Jetta of yours does look like a drugmobile."

"Really? How's that?"

Minty shrugged. "No offense, but it's the kind of vehicle the owner won't mind that much if it's impounded."

"I'd mind. It's the only car I own."

Jimmy Minty looked like he could just kick himself. "Damn. I guess I hurt your feelings."

"Not at all." Miles smiled.

The other man puzzled over how this could be for several full beats. "You want to know a secret?"

The honest answer to this was no, so Miles said nothing.

"What you were doing over there yesterday? I do the same thing, sometimes."

"What's that?"

"You know. Just drive over, sit in the car and try to figure it all out."

"All *what* out?" Miles asked, genuinely curious.

Minty shrugged. "Life, I guess. The way things turn out. I guess some people would think it's pretty weird, me ending up a cop."

"Not me, Jimmy."

Minty studied him carefully, perhaps suspecting an insult. "My dad and all, is what I meant. It's true. He did slap my mom around a little. That's what you meant a minute ago, right? And I guess we did have a freezer full of meat out back that wasn't always taken in season. Shit like that. But I miss him anyway. You only get one father, is the way I look at it, even though now, looking back, I can see where he crossed the line. Anyway, a cop's what I turned out to be, weird or not. God probably had a hand in it, I guess."

"I suppose it's possible."

Jimmy nodded. "Take you. If your mother hadn't got sick when she did, you probably never would have come back here at all, am I right?"

Miles allowed that this, too, was possible.

"That's what I mean. Sometimes I drive over to the old neighborhood and just sit there." He paused. "I always think about your ma. Pretty awful way for anybody to die."

"Can we change the subject?" Miles said.

"Hell, yeah." Jimmy Minty straightened up and shook his head. "I don't know what got me started on all this. Seeing you just sitting there yesterday, I guess, and thinking how we used to be friends. All that water over the dam. How's that cute little girl of yours?"

"Good," Miles told him. "Happier than she's been in a while." Since she stopped going out with your son was what Miles *didn't* say.

If Jimmy Minty intuited the omission he gave no sign. "Want to know another secret? I gotta think my Zack's still a little sweet on her," he said, letting the words hang in the air between them, as if inviting Miles to betray either enthusiasm or aversion. "Of course, with kids you never know. I told him at the time he should have let her down gentler. Treat people the way you want to be treated, is my motto. You can't go too far wrong. Not that you can tell kids their age anything."

Hearing the men's room door open behind him, Miles allowed himself a half smile. Few social situations were improved by Max Roby's participation, but this was one of them.

"I keep telling him if he doesn't start paying attention to his grades, no college is going to want him, but no, he's got all that figured out, just like they all do. Not that I blame him, exactly. He looks at me, and I'm doing all right without college—hell, better than all right, really—so he figures what the hell."

Jimmy Minty paused again. "What our kids don't understand is we want even *better* for them, not just as good. Am I right?"

Max's return spared Miles the necessity of agreeing with him.

"Jimmy Minty," said Max, sitting down on the bench seat and forcing the policeman to slide down next to the window. Max looked at him with what appeared to be total bewilderment. "My *God*, what a stupid kid you were growing up."

"Go easy, Dad," Miles said. "He's carrying a gun these days."

"I just hope he's smarter than he was back then," Max said, offering a paw to the policeman. "How the hell are you, Jimmy?"

Minty looked at the proffered hand as if he doubted Max had washed it in the men's room, but shook it anyway. "How you doin', Mr. Roby?"

Speaking to Miles now, as he and Jimmy Minty shook, Max said, "You remember what a stupid kid he was? My *God*, it was pitiful. I don't think I can remember another child so untalented."

Minty seemed to want his hand back now, but didn't know how to get it, and Miles shrugged at him as if to suggest he had no idea what possessed his father to act the way he did.

"It was enough to make you cry," Max said, finally letting go of the man's hand.

Minty seemed to be weighing the dangers and benefits of asking just what he'd done to warrant such a low opinion.

"I suppose it should be a lesson to us all," Max observed. "Never give up on a child. 'Cause even the ones you have to tie their shoes for on their wedding day could surprise you and end up gainfully employed."

Max, with a face almost beatific, delivered this lesson as if to suggest he meant the whole thing as a compliment, causing the officer to knit his brow in confusion. He was *almost* sure he was being insulted, but not quite.

Miles, of course, had often seen his father smile and chuckle and slap men on the back, continuing to insult them until they finally had no choice but to punch him. Only the smartest popped him right away. Once Max had established that whatever he said was all in good fun, it was hard to break free of that context. Miles also knew that the target of his father's ridicule often turned on a dime, so he wasn't surprised when it did so now.

"My son here is the opposite," Max explained. "Always at the top of his class . . . straight A's right through school. You'd have sworn he'd go places."

Miles sighed, resigned to his inevitable drubbing. Before, Max had insulted Jimmy Minty while looking at Miles. Now, insulting his son, he was, of course, speaking directly at the previous object of his scorn.

"There's nothing harder to figure than a kid," Max was telling him, as if he'd spent the better part of a long, largely contemplative life studying this question. "I'd have bet that Miles here would have grown up to have a good heart. If his father was on his uppers and needed a hand and asked his own son for a job, he'd help pronto. But apparently not."

"You about ready to go, Dad?"

"No, I'm talking to Jimmy Minty. Go ahead if you want."

Miles caught the eye of the waitress and signaled for the check.

"Jimmy here may not have been gifted like you, but I bet you he understands what I'm saying."

Minty's brow furrowed even deeper at this second reference to his intellectual limitations, even though Max had safely located these in the past.

"You see, Jimmy, I asked my son to let me help him paint our old church, so I'd have the money to go down to the Keys, but for some reason he won't hire me. I can still climb like a monkey, too."

Having slid a five-dollar bill onto the table, Miles stood to go. "You're sure you don't want a lift home, Dad? I'm not coming back for you, so don't bother calling me at the restaurant."

"I don't intend to call you," his father assured him. "Besides, Jimmy Minty here can give me a lift in the cruiser."

"Actually, that's against the rules," Minty said. He was looking even more boxed in now that Miles had vacated his side of the booth. That left him and Max sitting way too close, and he knew how this would look to other people, two men crammed together like that on the same side of a small booth, one of them with crumbs in his beard.

"Hell, I can understand that," Max conceded, waving good riddance to Miles and looking like a man who had no intention of moving. "Rules are rules. They may be dumb, and the people you hire to enforce them may be dumber yet, but what can you do? The law's the law. There's no law says a man's own son can't help him out when he needs it, that's all I'm saying. Ain't no law against that."

OUTSIDE, Miles got into the car and turned the key in the ignition, determined to ignore the knocking on the window of the donut shop. His father, having made his point, now decided to unmake it, since the truth was that he probably *did* want a lift somewhere. Besides, he hadn't hit Miles up for a loan yet. Sitting in the Jetta, pretending not to hear the frantic knocking, Miles supposed he understood his father's thinking better than Max did himself. The thing to do was put the car in reverse, back out of the parking space and drive off. Teach the old man a lesson. Maybe because he was grateful to Max for giving Jimmy Minty such a hard time, he gave up the pretense and acknowledged hearing the knocking on the window. He was immediately glad that he did, for the scene framed in the window was priceless. In order to rap on the glass, Max had to lean across the booth in such a way that his moist, fragrant armpit was practically covering the policeman's face. Miles couldn't help but smile. He *was* grateful for his father's existence, just as Minty had told him he should be. Sighing, he waved for Max to come along, which the old man would do, Miles knew, in his own sweet time.

His feet flat on the floor beside the Jetta's pedals, Miles felt some give in the metal beneath the worn carpet, which suggested that the

"It was enough to make you cry," Max said, finally letting go of the man's hand.

Minty seemed to be weighing the dangers and benefits of asking just what he'd done to warrant such a low opinion.

"I suppose it should be a lesson to us all," Max observed. "Never give up on a child. 'Cause even the ones you have to tie their shoes for on their wedding day could surprise you and end up gainfully employed."

Max, with a face almost beatific, delivered this lesson as if to suggest he meant the whole thing as a compliment, causing the officer to knit his brow in confusion. He was *almost* sure he was being insulted, but not quite.

Miles, of course, had often seen his father smile and chuckle and slap men on the back, continuing to insult them until they finally had no choice but to punch him. Only the smartest popped him right away. Once Max had established that whatever he said was all in good fun, it was hard to break free of that context. Miles also knew that the target of his father's ridicule often turned on a dime, so he wasn't surprised when it did so now.

"My son here is the opposite," Max explained. "Always at the top of his class . . . straight A's right through school. You'd have sworn he'd go places."

Miles sighed, resigned to his inevitable drubbing. Before, Max had insulted Jimmy Minty while looking at Miles. Now, insulting his son, he was, of course, speaking directly at the previous object of his scorn.

"There's nothing harder to figure than a kid," Max was telling him, as if he'd spent the better part of a long, largely contemplative life studying this question. "I'd have bet that Miles here would have grown up to have a good heart. If his father was on his uppers and needed a hand and asked his own son for a job, he'd help pronto. But apparently not."

"You about ready to go, Dad?"

"No, I'm talking to Jimmy Minty. Go ahead if you want."

Miles caught the eye of the waitress and signaled for the check.

"Jimmy here may not have been gifted like you, but I bet you he understands what I'm saying."

Minty's brow furrowed even deeper at this second reference to his intellectual limitations, even though Max had safely located these in the past.

"You see, Jimmy, I asked my son to let me help him paint our old

"No," she admitted. "You're just the only one who hits it every time."

When she stepped away, the policeman shrugged. "Hey, Miles. I thought that was your Jetta out there. You should've spent the extra for the undercoating. What would it have run you—couple hundred?"

It never took Jimmy Minty long to turn any conversation to one about money. He particularly liked to draw Miles's attention to whatever was wrong with any of his possessions, such as rust on the Jetta, of which there was plenty. Miles had long suspected that Jimmy Minty considered him some kind of yardstick by which he might measure his own economic well-being. The oddest thing about this, Miles thought, was that it seemed a direct extension of their childhoods on Long Street. Jimmy Minty had always taken careful inventory of Miles's belongings, wanting to know how much everything cost and where it was purchased. If they got similar Christmas presents, Jimmy liked to explain why his was better, that it had been purchased smarter and cheaper because *his* dad knew where to go—even if the toy in question was obviously a cheap knockoff. After detailing the advantages of his present, he'd suggest they switch, just for a while; often, before Jimmy returned it, Miles's toy would get broken.

Even thirty years later Miles could still remember the relief he felt when his mother took him out of the public grade school and enrolled him at Sacred Heart, where Jimmy—the family was not Catholic—could not follow. Gradually, though they remained neighbors, the boys' lives began to drift apart, and by the time they were thrown together again in high school, they had different lives, different friends. Of course, Jimmy's, as he explained to Miles, were better. After graduation he did a stint in the service while Miles was away at college, and by the time Miles returned to Empire Falls, Jimmy was newly married and living in Fairhaven. He visited his parents, though, and after Miles and Janine got married he made overtures about striking up their old friendship, something Miles didn't particularly desire, since the grown-up Jimmy Minty had the same way of taking inventory behind his eyes, only now he was comparing wives. For the last decade, they had seldom seen each other, except in moving vehicles or when Jimmy had a new toy he wanted to show off in the Empire Grill. The last time—a year ago—he'd ordered a steak and then lingered at the counter drinking coffee until Miles deigned to notice the red Camaro parked out front. On any such occasion Jimmy would assure Miles that he was doing all right for himself, despite having been denied opportunities like college. If he kept his nose clean, he didn't see any reason he shouldn't be the next chief of police of Empire Falls. His son, Zack, though—*he* was going to have it made.

"That your dad I saw with you?" Jimmy wondered now, nodding toward the men's room.

"You know it was. You sat right there"— Miles nodded through the window at the cruiser—"staring at us."

"The light was reflecting off the glass," Minty said. "It could've been anybody."

"Hell of a guess, then."

"Sorry about yesterday," he said, apparently in reference to the young police officer who had interrogated Miles on Long Street. "New kid. Still learning the ropes. Good thing I happened by, though. You talk back to him or something?"

"Not even remotely."

Minty shrugged. "Well, you pissed him off somehow. Good thing I turned up when I did."

This second reference to his good fortune, Miles realized, was intended as another chance for Miles to express his gratitude. That he should fail to take advantage of it was visibly disappointing, but Jimmy seemed determined to get over it.

"Breaks your heart, doesn't it?" he said. "The old neighborhood?"

Miles tried to navigate their talk into the calmer waters of generality. "The whole town, for that matter."

Jimmy Minty's surprised, even hurt expression suggested that he considered this indictment of Empire Falls far too sweeping. "I still like it here," he said. "I can't help it, I just do. People say there are better places, but I don't know." He paused in case Miles wanted to rattle off a list of supposedly better places. "Long Street, though. That's different. I get called up there all the time these days. Nothing but wife beaters and drug dealers anymore."

"Wife beaters aren't anything new," Miles reminded him, since Jimmy's own father, William, had been known to settle marital differences in this fashion.

Jimmy ignored him. "Hell, the place you were parked out front of is the biggest drug house in town." He lowered his voice now. "We've been monitoring who goes in and out for a while. I guess Officer Pollard thought you were there to make a score."

Miles couldn't help smiling. "Somebody should tell him he'll have rust was eating away at the chassis. Minty was right about that, too; he should've sprung for the undercoating. As he watched the two men slide out of the booth, he realized that Jimmy Minty hadn't been telling the truth about light reflecting off the donut shop window. Everything on the other side of the glass possessed the stark clarity of an Edward Hopper painting, which meant that Jimmy had pretended to be unable to see what had been plainly visible. A silly lie. A lie so small and to so little purpose that it suggested to Miles a way of life, a strategy for confronting the world, and this was further reason—if any was needed—to doubt the truth of everything the man had said inside. As Minty paid the bill at the register and Max bought a pack of cigarettes from the machine, Miles tasted something on the back of his tongue. Too much coffee mingling with stomach acid, probably. Either that or anger mingling with fear. Miles swallowed hard, forcing down whatever it was.

The two men pushed through the door onto the sidewalk, and Miles noticed that both had acquired toothpicks. "You're okay, Jimmy," Miles heard his father say. "I'll tell you the God's honest truth. I'd rather have a complete idiot for a son than an ingrate."

Instead of getting into the cruiser, Minty came around the Jetta and motioned for Miles to roll down the window. "Take a little walk with me," he suggested, his voice low, confidential.

"I really need to get back to the restaurant," Miles told him.

"Won't take a minute."

"Go ahead," Max said. "I'll just sit here by myself and wait. You go with Jimmy Minty and swap secrets."

Miles followed the policeman over to his patrol car, where he rolled the toothpick in his mouth as if considering how to begin. "I shouldn't be doing this, but we go back a long ways," he said. "I was going to mention it back inside, but then your old man came back and I didn't want to worry him."

"What is it, Jimmy?"

"Here's the deal," Minty said, working his toothpick. "There's a lot of dope around town right now. Tell your brother to be careful."

Miles felt himself instantly bristle, more at the presumed intimacy than the implied accusation. "Why should David be careful?"

"Hey. I understand. He's your brother. I'm just saying."

"No, Jimmy. *What* are you saying?"

"I'm just . . . nothing. Forget it. I'm just saying. Word to the wise is all."

The toothpick still twirled thoughtfully. Miles considered grabbing it and running it through the man's bottom lip and tying it there in a splintered knot. "And I can't help thinking how bad your ma would feel if—"

Rather than punch an armed cop in broad daylight in the middle of Empire Avenue, Miles turned on his heel and strode back to the Jetta. The suddenness of this movement apparently caught his father by surprise as he was rummaging through the Jetta's glove box. This discovery had the unintended effect of sending Miles back to Jimmy Minty, who hadn't moved. "Look," he said, "you don't know the first thing about my mother, okay, so don't bring her up in any more conversations."

"Hey—"

"No. Shut up and listen, Jimmy," Miles said, feeling his fury rise in his throat—the taste was anger, after all, not fear—and the blood pounding in his cheeks. "You . . . didn't . . . know . . . her. Say it for me, so I know you understand."

Jimmy Minty's face had gone pale. "Hey, okay. I didn't really know your mother."

"Fine," Miles said, some of the rage draining out of him, replaced by the knowledge that he'd overreacted. "Terrific."

"You shouldn't tell me to shut up, Miles," Minty said. "Not out here in public like this. This uniform entitles me to some respect."

"You're right," Miles admitted, flushed with shame yet unwilling to surrender his anger. "You're right, and I'm sorry. Just don't pretend you knew my mother."

"Hey, I thought she was a great lady. That's all I was saying—" But he must have seen Miles's color rising again, because he stopped. "Your brother should be careful is all I'm saying, okay? Everybody knows he's growing marijuana out there in—"

"See?" Miles said. "That's where you're wrong. Everybody does *not* know that. *I* don't know that, for instance." Which was true. He didn't know it, not for sure.

"How come you're getting so bent outta shape, Miles? I try to do you and your brother a favor—"

"No," Miles interrupted him, feeling suddenly calm. "I don't believe that. I have no idea what you're trying to do, Jimmy. I don't know why I'm suddenly seeing you everywhere I turn lately. I don't know why my name should come up in your conversation with Mrs. Whiting at the courthouse, either . . . "

Minty squinted at this, then glanced away.

"But I do know you aren't looking out for my well-being. That much I'm sure of. So from now on, if you want to do me a favor, stay away from me and my family. That goes for your kid too. There are lots of girls in Empire Falls. As far as I'm concerned he can choose any one he likes. There's just one he can't have, and that's Tick."

A sly smile began to steal over the policeman's features, and Miles turned away, fearing the temptation to remove it.

"How come you don't like me, Miles?" Minty called after him. "I've always wondered why."

Miles answered without turning around. "Call it the habit of a lifetime."

Back in the Jetta, Miles waited to turn the key in the ignition until Minty's cruiser disappeared down the avenue.

"*God*, what a prize dunce he was," Max recalled fondly.

"He wasn't stupid, Dad. He was sneaky and mean and envious and dangerous. He still is."

"Don't get mad at me," his father said. "It's Jimmy Minty you're mad at. I'm just a useless old man."

Miles put the car in reverse. "Did you find what you were looking for in the glove box?"

"I borrowed ten dollars," his father said sheepishly. "I was going to mention it, but you never gave me the chance."

"Right."

"I was," Max insisted, perhaps truthfully. He did sometimes tell the truth if it suited his purpose. "If you'd hire me, I wouldn't have to be broke all the while. If I could make some money, you'd get rid of me for the winter."

Before pulling out, Miles craned his neck forward to look down Empire Avenue, to make sure no traffic was coming. When he and his mother used to walk downtown for a Saturday matinee at the old Bijou Theater, the sidewalks had been so crowded, the street so clogged with vehicles, that pedestrians had to turn sideways to pass by one another. They crossed the street between cars backed up for blocks from the traffic light. Now Empire Avenue was empty all the way down to the old shirt factory (NO TRESPASSING WITHOUT PERMISSION) where Miles's mother had worked so they could afford the rent on the little house on Long Street, in the dark upper bedroom of which, after her cancer returned the final time, she'd screamed her agony so loudly the neighbors could hear her. Of *course* Jimmy Minty had heard those screams.

Miles himself had heard them all the way down in Portland, in his small Catholic college, and hearing them he'd hurried home, even though she'd begged him not to.

Looking down the deserted street, Miles couldn't help feeling that everyone in town must have heard her terrible screams. His brother, a mere boy, had fled into the bottle, his father to the Florida Keys. It was almost possible to believe her screams were responsible for the mass exodus that by now had lasted more than two decades, a panicky flight from her pain that emptied out the town.

"You can drop me off at Callahan's," Max suggested.

Miles blinked, then turned to stare at his father. "You mean Callahan's right there?" he said, pointing at the red-brick tavern across the street, his mother-in-law's place.

"Right."

"For *that* you wanted a lift?"

"Maybe I wanted to spend some time with my son. Or is there some law against that, too?"

Miles sighed. The old man was truly without conscience.

"How come you've got a Martha's Vineyard real estate guide in there?" his father wondered, pointing at the glove box.

"Is there a law against that?" Miles said.

Max ignored this. "Be just like you to move to some island and leave me here without a job. I ever wanted to see you, I'd have to swim."

"I'm not going anywhere, Dad. You said so yourself," Miles reminded him. "It was just a week's vacation."

"You *could've* taken me along, you know. I might like a vacation myself. Did that ever occur to you?"

Miles pulled across the street into Callahan's parking lot

When his father started to get out, Miles said, "Dad, you've still got crumbs in your beard."

"So what?" said Max, closing the door on the possibility of enlightenment.

[CHAPTER 6]

"I DON'T THINK Mrs. Roderigue likes my snake," Tick confessed to her father.

It was a Thursday in mid-September, and on Thursday nights she and Miles always had dinner together, since Janine usually worked the desk at the fitness club until eight and Tick refused to eat with the Silver Fox. At the Empire Grill, Thursday nights also meant Chinese. Tonight David had on special something called Twice-Cooked Noodles with Scallops in *Hoisin* Sauce. His brother's more adventurous concoctions always made Miles smile in memory of old Roger Sperry, whose favorite special had always been Deep-Fried Haddock with Tartar Sauce, Whipped Potatoes with Beef Gravy, a side of Apple Sauce and Parker House Rolls. His theory of noodles, which Roger didn't often put into practice, was to leave them in boiling water until you were sure they were cooked; then you wouldn't need to cook them again. It was also his firm conviction that there wasn't much point in fighting a world war if you were going to come home and start serving things in *hoisin* sauce—whatever that was. That was the sort of thing you'd do if you lost the damn war. (Roger would never have made a distinction between the Japanese, with whom we'd been engaged in armed conflict, and the Chinese, with whom we had not.)

Miles himself had had some doubts about International Nights when his brother first proposed them as part of his plan to attract out-of-town business—something they'd have to do if the restaurant were going to survive the local economy. For a while Friday and Saturday nights didn't show a profit, but David had correctly predicted that good, cheap ethnic food would eventually attract students and junior faculty from Fairhaven, who would consider the grill's worn-out, cigarette-burned countertop and wobbly booths "honest" or "retro" or some damn thing. Tonight was only the second Thursday they'd served Chinese—to augment their Friday Italian and Saturday Mexican—and Miles was pleased to see the restaurant nearly full of people, many of them new faces, who seemed willing to entertain the possibility that noodles might benefit from a second cooking. When a brief lull occurred, David turned away from the stove, leaned on his spatula and searched out Miles's eye, raising an eyebrow. Not bad? Miles nodded. Not bad.

In fact, tonight it all seemed better than "not bad." Granted, his first week back from the Vineyard had been tough, but it usually was. Every year he left the island haunted by a profound feeling of personal failure. Was it the island itself that inspired this? Perhaps. More likely it had something to do with Peter and Dawn, who, without intending to, reminded him of who he'd wanted to be when they had all been students together. Of course it was possible that they too were haunted by similar regrets. After all, back when they were undergraduates, Peter had wanted to be a playwright, Dawn a poet. Certainly the way they talked about their profession in television suggested they also wondered if they hadn't betrayed their original, deeper purpose. Maybe they even indulged the feeling, as Miles sometimes did, that they each must have a double in some parallel universe, happily living the life they'd imagined for themselves in their youth.

But such self-indulgence was fraudulent. For one thing, Miles couldn't even be sure anymore if this alternate life was one he'd imagined or just one he'd inherited from his mother's hopes and wishes. From the time he was a boy, he would look up from a book he was reading to find her quietly studying him. "My little scholar," she'd say, smiling. Later, in college, he'd been greatly attracted to the exciting life his professors seemed to lead, richly furnished with books and ideas worth arguing over, and he'd thought that maybe his mother was right, that the life of the mind was his own truest destiny. One thing was for sure. He'd never aspired to feeding other professors twice-cooked noodles for a living.

Over at the counter Charlene was balancing plates up her forearm, and at this distance she might almost have been the girl he'd had a crush on in high school, a girl so womanly at age eighteen that she made Miles, at fifteen, feel about eleven. Looking at her now made it hard for him to claim he'd been an entirely unwilling participant in his own foiled destiny. Yes, he'd been attracted to the life of the mind, and no doubt his mother's idea of the man she thought he would become had shaped his own image of himself, but when she'd fallen ill and he'd left school to return to Empire Falls and manage the grill for Mrs. Whiting, his doing so had not been entirely altruistic. True, he'd wanted to be near his mother; and yes, his brother was already exhibiting signs of trouble. But he'd also thought of Charlene, calculating that the three years' age difference wouldn't matter so much now, at twenty-one and twenty-four. Though he told Mrs. Whiting he wanted to mull over her offer, by the time he'd hung up the phone he'd already decided. That summer Charlene's first husband had run off and left her, and Miles had thought maybe . . . just maybe. What he had no way of knowing then was that by the time he returned to Empire Falls, Charlene would already be engaged to husband number two.

No, he certainly had not been an unwilling participant. And, more to the point, if given an opportunity to rewrite the script, he would not be inclined to do so. At least not tonight, in this restaurant that would one day be his, sharing a booth with his daughter, whose destiny would *not* be tied to Empire Falls—not if he had anything to say about it. That his mother had believed the same thing about his own destiny was vaguely disconcerting, but tonight he couldn't help feeling fortunate. For the first time in a decade, business was looking up. David appeared to have banished the worst of his demons. Tick, it seemed, would survive the divorce. There was much to be thankful for, even if the balance of things remained too precarious to inspire confidence, so on nights like this one his life seemed almost . . . almost enough.

"BUT HERE'S THE THING," Tick was saying, using her fork as a baton to emphasize a point about her art teacher. Miles, studying the fork, was grateful that, unlike her grandfather, Tick was able to demonstrate ideas without flinging food. "What if she *did* like it? That'd be even worse. I mean, if she *liked* it, then I'd wonder what was wrong with it."

Miles tried to suppress a smile but couldn't. His daughter's grasp of adult situations often staggered him. In this instance, she understood completely what the endorsement of a fool was worth. Miles had gone to high school with Doris Roderigue—Doris Flynn, back then—and he knew her mind had fused shut sometime during Catholic grade school. Nothing had happened since she was twelve that did anything except reinforce the convictions she already held. As a condition for keeping her job, the school district insisted that she attend summer school in Farmington, but these classes did little to shake the woman's defiant convictions, which she proudly maintained were uncorrupted by the university.

In Bill Roderigue, a local insurance man, she'd found her ideal mate, an infinitely patient fellow who never seemed to weary of her sense of thwarted superiority. Miles, after serving several terms on the school board, knew most of Tick's teachers and made it a matter of policy not to speak ill of them, regardless of how ignorant and narrow-minded they were, but with Doris Roderigue he was often tempted to make an exception. During the last five years he'd run up against her on numerous occasions—about curriculum, about books held in the library, about staffing—but since the day he'd invited her, in public meeting, to explain a single difference between the work of Andrew Wyeth and Jackson Pollock and then used her startled confusion to suggest an explanation for why art history was not included in her courses, she'd steered clear of him. According to Tick, the woman was steering clear of her as well, by putting her at the table composed of the least motivated students in the class and then pretending the table didn't exist.

"Keep in mind," Miles reminded her, "it's not you she objects to, it's me. She probably thinks I'm trying to get her fired."

"Are you?"

"Teachers can't be fired unless they molest their students," Miles told her. "Doris hasn't been molesting anybody, has she?"

But Tick had turned her attention back to her dinner, pushing the ingredients around on her plate thoughtfully, as if considering a better, more artistic use for food.

"Has she made any specific criticisms of your snake?"

"*That's* the thing," Tick said happily, again wielding her fork as a baton. Lately all her statements were preceded by variations on "the thing." Here's the thing. That's the thing. The thing is. "I think what she doesn't like about *my* snake is that it reminds her of *real* snakes."

"That's one possibility," Miles agreed. The other that occurred to him was more Freudian, though he didn't think his teenage daughter needed to start worrying about sexual repression just yet.

"Which is interesting," Tick went on, "because it means that the better I draw the snake, the more it will remind her of what she hates, and the worse grade I'll get. Hence"—this word was another of Tick's new rhetorical devices—"if I want a good grade, my strategy should be to draw the snake *badly*."

"Or not draw a snake," Miles felt compelled to point out.

"Except our assignment was to draw our most vivid dream, and that's my most vivid dream."

"I understand," Miles said. "But you mistrust your teacher's judgment about the merits of your snake, correct?"

"Correct."

"Hence"—Miles grinned—"you might as well distrust the wisdom of the assignment, right? Draw her an angel. Mrs. Roderigue would be cheered to think you're dreaming of angels." This was no guess, either. Doris Roderigue, who'd never seen the sense of separating church and state, openly encouraged work with religious themes.

"But I'm dreaming of snakes."

"What you're dreaming about is none of her business," Miles pointed out, a little surprised by his growing anger at the thought of trusting the development of his daughter, or any smart kid for that matter, to the likes of Doris Roderigue.

"Want to know what your real problem is?" said Charlene, who had passed their booth several times during this conversation and apparently overheard enough to feel qualified to contribute. Charlene hadn't been a small-town waitress all her life for nothing. She entered into the conversations of diners with both confidence and a sense of entitlement. Last spring David and Miles had each suggested this might not be a good idea with their new evening clientele, especially with the professors, who probably weren't accustomed to having their thinking clarified by waitresses. Nor were they likely to tip anyone who'd belittled their logic. Charlene had briefly considered the wisdom of this advice, but in the end rejected it. For one thing, she said, having listened to their conversations, many of the professors badly needed a little clarification. For another, she was confident that despite their carefully trimmed beards, their pressed chinos and tweed jackets, college professors tipped in the same fashion as other men—according to cup size. She was doing very well by them, thanks all the same. "Your *real* problem," she told Tick, "is that you're dreaming instead of eating. Shall we let your father in on your secret?"

"The thing is"—Tick began, pointing the tines of her fork at Charlene, who surprised both father and daughter by snatching the fork and pointing it back at Tick, who leaned away in mock fear.

"And don't give me 'the thing is.'"

"What secret?" Miles said.

Charlene handed the fork back to Tick, then put her hands on her hips and regarded him as you would a favored pet, perhaps a dog that's found a place in your heart even though you've owned other, smarter dogs. "The purpose of this whole conversation has been to distract you from the obvious fact that Tick isn't eating her dinner. Again."

In addition to feeling free to enter into the conversations of her customers, Charlene, a full-service waitress, never shirked from reminding people that there was no excuse for wasting good food when other people were going hungry. She was particularly vigilant with Tick, who after her checkup last spring was declared underweight. Not that Tick was the only one whose eating habits drew Charlene's notice and comment. She'd been on Miles's case for years, pointing out his tendency to pick listlessly at things instead of sitting down to a proper meal. Over the years he'd fallen into the classic restaurateur's trap of eating his mistakes—the extra order of fries, the under- or overcooked burger—and not just when he was hungry but whenever they occurred. Tonight, for instance, that bowl of David's bisque, simply because it finished off the pot. It was Charlene's opinion that if Miles could bring himself to toss out every stray french fry that fell onto the counter, he'd weigh no more than his brother, David, who was gaunt and sinewy.

"It's not nice to tell a person's secrets, Charlene." Tick frowned. "I don't go around telling your secrets."

"That shows you're smart," Charlene said.

"She hasn't done that bad a job," Miles said weakly, indicating Tick's plate. True, she'd flattened out her food, artfully carving out an area in the middle to suggest that where there had once been food, there now was none. Still, Miles guessed that at least a third of the portion David had served her was gone.

"No, Miles," Charlene said. "*You're* the one who hasn't done such a bad job. You ate your own bisque and for the last fifteen minutes you've been picking at Tick's dinner. Don't tell me you haven't, either, because I've been watching you."

Well, it was true Miles *had* been picking at his daughter's food a little—surprised, as always, by how tasty David's specials were.

"I can't help it if I'm not hungry, Charlene," Tick said, pushing her plate away now that there was no point in continuing the charade. "It's not a person's fault if they're not hungry."

Charlene pushed the plate back in front of her. "Yes, it is," she said. "That's exactly whose fault it is. Kate Moss is yesterday's news, kid. Eat."

When she was gone, Tick speared a small *hoisin*-covered scallop and bit it in half, surrendering a half-guilty grin to her father.

"Charlene has secrets?" Miles said hopefully. It pleased him that she'd been watching him, hinting as it did at the possibility—admittedly remote—of an affection that transcended their long friendship. She'd been between boyfriends for some time, and Miles's divorce would soon be final, so maybe. And for years she'd been claiming that Miles was exactly the *sort* of man she'd fall in love with if she had any sense at all—a good man, straight and true, who, with the slightest encouragement would love her all the days of his life. So again, maybe.

Unfortunately, Charlene had also admitted, even after four failed marriages, her abiding preference for bad men whose insides were all twisted up in knots, and who cleared out the minute the going got tough. They had fast cars and drove them recklessly, and this was something she actually liked about them. There was no telling what would happen if she ever hooked up with a man like Miles, but she suspected she'd end up being mean to him, probably even meaner than Janine had been, which was going some. "I just don't think I could go through life at your speed, Miles," she told him once. "Don't you ever want to just put the pedal down to the floor and just see what it feels like?" Therefore, probably not.

"Everybody has secrets except you, Daddy," Tick was saying.

Miles considered this, then said, "What makes you think I don't have a few?"

His daughter didn't answer right away. "It's not like you don't have any," she explained, for once leaving her fork at rest. "It's just that everybody figures them out."

"I think you're just repeating what your mother always says about me."

"I'm repeating what *everybody* says about you. Because it's true. I'm more like Mom," she added somberly, as if this were something she wasn't particularly proud of. Since he and Janine had filed for divorce, Tick had begun cataloging her differences and similarities to each of her parents, perhaps thinking this genetic road map might make her own destiny more navigable. "I'll be good at keeping secrets. If I cheated on my husband, nobody would ever know."

Miles opened his mouth, then shut it again, wondering as he often did if there was another sixteen-year-old like this one anywhere else in the world. "Tick," he finally said.

"I didn't say I'd cheat on my husband," she added. "I just said I can keep a secret."

Before Miles could respond, the bell above the front door tinkled and Janine materialized in the doorway, as if summoned by her daughter's allusion. Without pausing for a moment, she headed right for them through the crowded restaurant. Tick, also without turning around in the booth, seemed to know that her mother had appeared, and she slid over next to the window to make room.

"We weren't expecting you for another hour, at least," Miles said when Janine slid into the booth, pulled her sweatshirt over her head and revealed a hot-pink exercise leotard underneath.

"Yeah, well, here I am, anyway," she said. "And don't be staring at my breasts, Miles. We were married for twenty years, and they never interested you that whole time."

Miles felt himself color, because he *had* been staring at them. "That's not true," he said weakly. Actually, he wasn't really all that interested in them now, except for the fact that they were so completely on display beneath her leotard—though this wasn't a subject he was keen on pursuing in front of their daughter.

"I just finished up at the club," Janine explained, "and I'm hot and sweaty and I haven't even had a chance to shower." She turned toward Tick. "You ready to go home?"

"I guess," Tick said.

"You guess," Janine repeated. "Is there somebody who'd know for sure? Somebody we could consult for a definitive answer?"

"I have to get my backpack," Tick told her. "You don't *have* to be such a bitch every minute, do you?"

"Yes, I do, little girl," Janine said, sliding out of the booth so Tick could get out. "You'll understand why when you're forty."

"You're forty-one," Tick reminded her. "Forty-two this January."

Miles watched his daughter all the way into the back room, feeling, as he always did these days, a terrible mix of irreconcilable emotions—the shame of his failed marriage, anger at Janine for her part in its dissolution, anger at himself for his own part, and gratitude that they'd managed to be faithful to a bad idea long enough to have this child. He would've liked to know if Janine felt any of this, or whether she'd managed to simplify her emotional life by indulging only the regret. Turning back to Janine, Miles caught her sneaking a scallop off Tick's plate.

"Damn," she said, aware that she'd been witnessed. "*Damn*, that's good."

"I could order you some, Janine," Miles offered. "It wouldn't kill you to eat something."

"That's where you're mistaken, Miles. That's exactly what it would do. I'm *not* going to be fat again, not ever."

Charlene happened to be passing by at that moment, so Janine handed her the plate. "Do me a favor and get this away from me, will you?" she said, then turned back to Miles. "There's a word for people like you," she continued. "'Enabler.'"

There was a word for people like Janine, too, Miles thought, and her own daughter had already applied it.

"You're through feeding me, buddy boy. I've assumed control of my own body."

"Good," Miles said. "I'm happy for you."

If Janine heard any sarcasm in this, she didn't react to it. In fact, some of her anger seemed to leak away, and when Tick reappeared with her backpack, Janine said, "Why don't you go on out to the car for a couple minutes. Since I'm here, I want to talk to your father."

Tick leaned into the booth to give Miles a kiss. "See you tomorrow, Daddy. Will you have time to proof a paper?"

"I'll make time," Miles said. "It wasn't very nice to fool me about eating your dinner, though."

"I know," she said without the slightest indication of remorse. "You're just so easy."

Once she was safely through the door, Miles turned back to Janine. "You sure are tough on her lately." He knew, as soon as he spoke the words, that they were a mistake. For Miles, one of the great mysteries of marriage was that you had to actually say things before you realized they were wrong. Because he'd been saying the wrong thing to Janine for so many years, he'd grown wary, testing most of his observations in the arena of his imagination before saying them out loud, but even then he was often wrong. Of course, the other possibility was that there *was* no right thing to say, that the choice wasn't between right and wrong but between wrong, more wrong, and as wrong as you can get. Wrong, all of it, to one degree or another, by definition, or by virtue of the fact that Miles himself was the one saying it.

"Well, *somebody* has to be," Janine said, her hackles now as fully raised as her nipples. "Since she can do no wrong with either her father or her uncle."

Miles opened his mouth to object, but his wife—no surprise—wasn't finished.

"Walt's no better, either. The worse she treats him, the more he fawns over her."

"She's just a kid, Janine." Ours.

Janine picked up an unused spoon, held it like a knife at her temple and made as if to drive it home. "Miles. You're wrong. First, she's not a kid. You don't believe me, just look at her. Try using the eyes you look at other people with. Second, so what? I was never a kid and neither were you. From the time I was old enough to manage it, I was changing diapers. Tick's led a charmed life, and you know it."

"Wasn't that the idea?" Miles said. "I thought that's what we meant to do."

"Not forever, Miles."

What Miles was imagining right now was their daughter watching them, their heads bent forward toward the center of the table so they could lower their voices and still yell at each other. No, this last year of their daughter's life had been anything but charmed. Maybe the others hadn't been so wonderful either. "Janine," he said, feeling suddenly exhausted, "could we not fight?"

"Nope. That's what the last twenty years have been about, in case you missed it. Also, every time there's a problem and the damn school calls somebody, they don't call you, they call me. I'm the one who has to leave work to deal with it, not you."

"I'm not sure that's fair," Miles said. "I wish they *would* call me. If you'd let me have primary custody—"

"Right. And where would she live? Upstairs? Move the pallets of fryolator grease down to the basement to make a little room for her?"

"You have a point," Miles said, trying to keep the bitterness out of his voice. "I *am* left without a house in all this. Speaking of which."

"Don't." Janine pointed the spoon at him. "Don't go there."

"Okay," he agreed, since he'd already gone there and Janine knew it.

Janine had promised to talk to Walt about the house. The sensible, fair thing, she agreed, would be for Walt to buy out Miles's share—or what would have been his share if he had one. The settlement would award Janine the house and Miles had been instructed to continue paying half of the mortgage until such time as the property sold or she remarried. Privately, he and Janine had agreed that when the house did sell, they would divide what was left of the equity. The money they'd used for a down payment had been his, but it didn't amount to that much, and he'd decided not to make an issue of it, or anything else. His instructions to his lawyer had been simple: let her have what she wants. In truth, there was embarrassingly little to quibble over, and even if he'd felt like it, he couldn't be small with Janine without being small with Tick. Not an option.

However, the divorce would soon be final, allowing for Janine's long postponed nuptials, and Miles was beginning to wonder if he should have listened to his lawyer's advice. Walt Comeau, the lawyer had correctly predicted, would rent his own house and move in with Janine. "Is that what you want? For the man who stole your wife to live with her in *your* house, sleeping in *your* bed, all of it rent-free?" Well, of course Miles hadn't wanted that, but at the time such a scenario seemed far-fetched. What sort of man would behave that way? But then Miles wouldn't have predicted that Walt Comeau would also become a regular at the grill, dropping in every afternoon to drink coffee and play gin with Horace and offer Miles business tips. Just today he'd suggested that Miles add an "e" to the word "Grill" to make the place sound classier. Every time Walt made one of his proposals, two things occurred to Miles. First, strange as it seemed, was that Walt's purpose was *not* to inspire Miles to homicide. Walt Comeau truly believed his suggestions to be valuable. And second, he was probably offering them in lieu of rent. Most people, Miles had come to understand, went about their business logically enough if you granted them a couple fundamental assumptions. No court had ordered Walt to pay rent on Miles's house, so he wouldn't. Still, he couldn't help but feel sorry for the man whose wife he'd stolen—fair and square, Walt would consider it, the better man having won—and so, even without obligation to do so, he would continue to look for little opportunities to make it up to Miles. In fact, he seemed increasingly determined to help out in any way he could. No doubt he thought his free advice was worth thousands of dollars, yet Miles stubbornly refused to implement any of it. What could you do? Talk about leading a horse to water. No, if Miles were to die in his sleep tonight, Walt would tell every last mourner that he'd tried everything he could think of to turn the Empire Grill into a profitable enterprise. Miles was a hell of a nice guy, he would conclude, but he had no head for business. Nothing about any of this would strike the Silver Fox as outrageous.

"I *did* speak to him about it," Janine finally said, staring at her reflection in the window. "He said . . ." Here she paused again, as if she herself could hardly credit what she was about to report. "He said he's not sure that real estate here is that good an investment right now."

"Really," Miles said. "He figured that out?"

"He says he doesn't want to tie up his money until he's sure about his next move."

"When will that be?"

"I don't know, Miles. I really don't," she admitted, suddenly dropping the pretense of being angry. "Have you ever noticed the way he scratches his chin when he plays cards? When he's trying to figure out what Horace is holding? It's almost like time stops. Like you're watching a still life."

"Janine—"

"I mean, who knows? One minute he's talking about expanding the club, putting in more indoor tennis courts, then the next he's saying we should build a place out by the lake. There's a half acre of waterfront property he's had his eye on, but when I ask him where exactly, he gets all secretive, like I'm going to blab to somebody who'll buy it out from under him. Every time I try to pin him down about anything, he gets that sly expression, you know? The one he always gets right before Horace gins him."

"Janine."

She continued staring at her reflection, as if meeting his eye would amount to some terrible admission. When she finally did, there were tears, and it occurred to Miles that there might be something she wasn't telling him. Something she wasn't sure of herself.

"What, Miles?"

"Are you having second thoughts?"

She wiped the corner of one eye with the strap of her leotard and gathered her defiance again, causing Miles to wonder, as he had on and off for two decades, what there was about this combative stance that Janine found so attractive.

"No. Don't worry," she assured him. "I'm going through with it. I promise. This time next month all you'll owe is child support."

"I never said I wanted you to go through with anything," Miles reminded her, suddenly feeling the kind of tenderness toward his ex-wife that occasionally crept up on him when he wasn't paying strict attention.

"It's not Walt and me I'm worried about. What I still don't even begin to understand is us."

"You mean how we managed to make such a mess of everything?"

Janine made a face at him. "Hell, no, Miles. That part's easy. We messed things up because we didn't love each other. What I'd like to know is why. I mean, I told you why I didn't love you. Everything you did during the last twenty years that pissed me off, I told you about."

Miles couldn't help but smile. True, Janine's list of his shortcomings was long, comprehensive, and subject to constant revision.

"Now here we are almost divorced and I'm getting set to marry somebody else, and you still haven't told me why you didn't love me. Does that seem fair? I mean, if you were ever inclined to get married again—which I don't recommend—*you'd* at least know what to do different, right? Because I was honest with you."

"What do you want, Janine? A list of marital grievances? You took up with Walt Comeau, for God's sake."

"Well, sure, throw that in my face."

Now it was Miles's turn to study his reflection in the glass. The man who stared back at him looked exasperated.

"It's not fair, and you know it," she continued. "I mean, sure, fine. I took up with Walt, so you've got a gripe. But I took up with Walt because *you* didn't love me. I know it hurt your feelings, me falling in love with him, but you shouldn't pretend you were in love with me, Miles, because we both know you weren't."

"What's my part in this conversation? If you're going to speak for both of us—"

"Are you telling me you loved me, Miles? If that's what you want to tell me, say it. I'll shut up so you can." When he looked down at his hands, she said, "I didn't think so."

She was right, of course. In the deepest sense, he hadn't loved her. Not the way he'd intended to. Not as he'd sworn he would before God and family and friends, and this simple truth embarrassed him too deeply to allow for anything like analysis. No, he hadn't loved her, and he didn't know why. He also didn't know what to call whatever it was that would've prevented him from telling her, even if he had known. If you didn't call it love, what did you call the kind of affection that makes you want to protect someone from hurt? What was the name of the feeling that threatened to swamp him now, that made him want to take her in his arms and tell her that everything would be all right. If not love, then what?

Still, she was right. Because whatever it was he felt for this woman whose life had been joined to his for so long, whatever it was certainly couldn't be confused with desire and need and yearning. Miles knew that much, if only because he'd tried his best to confuse them.

"Why are you tormenting yourself, Janine?" he said. "If Walt makes you happy, what else matters?"

She studied him for a minute, then gave up. "Beats the shit out of me," she admitted, forcing a smile. "I guess I'd just like to hear you say I'm not a horrible person."

"I never said you were a—"

"That's what I'm trying to tell you, Miles," she said, sliding out of the booth. "You never said anything."

"HE KEEPS SAYING he can climb like a monkey," Miles told his brother. They were upstairs in his apartment above the restaurant, and it was nearly eleven o'clock. Miles, a lifelong insomniac, would be awake by five anyway, but he couldn't help resenting that if he *should* ever be visited by a decent night's sleep, he'd have to interrupt it to open the restaurant. David, who'd taken a small club soda from the mini-fridge, set it down on the floor and moved a huge box of toilet paper off the sofa so he'd have a place to sit. The Sox were on TV, a late game from the West Coast.

Janine had been right, of course. As things stood, there was no room for Tick here, even though he'd been toying with the idea earlier that evening, trying to make it work. He could move all the grill supplies back down into the basement until the river flooded again and the restaurant started taking on water. If he cleared out all that stuff, there would be room for both of them, except that a girl Tick's age needed more than space. She needed a room of her own with a door she could close, even slam, when necessary. Miles's apartment, which hadn't been occupied since Roger Sperry died, was basically one big room. Except for the door you entered by, there was only one other, to the bathroom, and even that didn't close tight. Tick deserved better. Sure, with a little work and expense he could make it nicer, but it would still be a shabby second-floor flat above a place of business.

For all of that, he knew that his daughter would jump at the chance to get out of her mother's house. She despised living under the same roof as Walt Comeau. Though it wasn't a whole lot bigger, the little cottage behind the bookstore on Martha's Vineyard would be plenty big for the two of them, if he could ever figure out how to afford it.

"Everything he does," David remarked from the sofa, "he does like a monkey." Regarding their father, David was unsentimental. "You're right not to let him on any ladders, though. Don't let him con you into feeling sorry for him."

"I'll try. But he's pretty good at getting to me. I guess I don't want to be sold short when I'm old," Miles said, trying to explain away the foolish emotion. Feeling sorry for Max Roby was certainly all of that.

"Pretty good night," David said, shaking his longish hair. The effect of wearing a hairnet through an eight-hour shift was that you looked like you were still wearing one even after you took it off.

"Better than pretty good," said Miles, who'd rung out the register. "Looks like Thursdays might fly."

"I'm not sure we've got our costs in line."

"I doubt we're too far off."

"You *do* know the next logical step, don't you?"

"Yes, I do," Miles said. This was an old conversation. Pointless, too, like so many of his conversations with his brother, going all the way back to when their mother was still alive. Strange. He and David were closer now, since his brother's crippling accident, than ever. Before, both men had pushed their conversations until their words burst into flame, rekindling age-old resentments, reopening old wounds. There was nearly a decade's difference in their ages, and their life experiences were radically dissimilar. Miles had grown up before their mother became ill, David after. Perhaps just as important, they'd always been temperamental opposites: Miles careful and thoughtful, like their mother; David energetic and restless, like Max. Since the accident, though, all this seemed to matter less, though it troubled Miles that their newfound intimacy seemed to depend on their having so little to say to each other. They passed the baton of the restaurant back and forth with an almost effortless minimum of talk. Often their communication seemed almost ritualistic. David would report to Miles that he'd locked up, understanding that Miles already knew this, but also that he expected to hear these words, probably was waiting to hear them, needing them to provide some kind of closure that the day wouldn't otherwise have.

"Wouldn't need to be a full liquor license," David said. "Beer and wine would do it."

"Mrs. Whiting won't go for it, though."

"She'd rather lose money?"

Odd, but Miles had the feeling this might be the precise, literal truth. It violated logic, of course. Why be content to squeak by on the slenderest of profit margins when there was an opportunity for more substantial gain? Mrs. Whiting was a practical and ruthless business-woman who had recognized the exact moment at which to sell each of the three Whiting mills, who had never before exhibited the slightest patience with borderline businesses. Yet for more than a decade she'd seemed content to let the Empire Grill limp along toward its inevitable extinction. In the absence of any other rational explanation, Miles had almost concluded that it must be a matter of affection. But for whom? Miles himself? It was possible, he supposed. Horace, as clever and cyn-ical an observer as the local scene offered, had concluded as much, so maybe. If not for Miles, for the Empire Grill itself? Unlikely, since the old woman hadn't set foot in its shabby premises in twenty years. The other possibility, which Miles kept returning to, was the old woman's fondness for Miles's mother, who had worked for Mrs. Whiting until she fell ill. So again, maybe.

"Reason with her," David urged him. "Tell her people won't eat spicy Mexican and Asian food without beer. And they like wine with Italian."

"I'll try," Miles said. "But don't get your hopes up. She's not stupid, but for some reason she doesn't like change. Maybe it's just old age. Maybe she doesn't want to be bothered. Anyway, it's her business."

David pondered this obvious truth while a Red Sox batter hit a tow-ering fly ball that was caught on the warning track. Then, studying his empty club soda, as if trying to recollect why a man like himself would drink soda water instead of beer, he said, "Want to hear another idea?"

No, was the simple truth. It had been a long day, and Miles was too tired and dispirited by his conversation with Janine to think. "Sure," he said. "What?"

"Go talk to your mother-in-law."

"Bea? Why?"

"Think about it, Miles. It makes sense."

"It's a thought," Miles said. Janine's mother owned not just the dying tavern, Callahan's, but the building in which the tavern was housed, which meant that Mrs. Whiting, if she felt betrayed and decided to be vindictive, would have little recourse. No, there was no need for David to explain his thinking here. If Mrs. Whiting didn't want to spring for a liquor license and give them a fighting chance, move the whole kit and caboodle across town. Bea's place was bigger, too, which meant they'd have room to grow.

"You'd be doing Bea a favor. She's going under by degrees. You could save her and yourself at the same time."

"I don't have the money to buy her place, David."

"Offer to go partners. She provides the liquor license, you provide the food service."

"And what do I do when you leave?"

"Am I going somewhere?"

"Well."

"Don't 'well' me, Miles."

"You get bored with things. And then you split. I don't mean that as a criticism. There's no reason you shouldn't. You don't have a family. I just don't have the luxury, is all."

"So you're saying I'm the reason you won't consider Bea's place?"

"I'm not saying I won't consider it," Miles said. "I admit, it's a thought."

"I wish you wouldn't say it like that," David told him. "It sounds dead already."

Miles didn't respond right away, not until he could speak without irritation. When the last Red Sox batter of the inning finally struck out with men on first and third, Miles said, "I owe her, David."

"Owe who?"

"Mrs. Whiting. Isn't that who we were talking about? Maybe Janine and Tick and I haven't had a terribly prosperous life, but it hasn't been bad, either. The restaurant has struggled, obviously, and God knows we've struggled right along with it, but we've kept our heads above water, and that's more than you can say for a lot of people around here. Mrs. Whiting could've closed the place down years ago, and where would that have left us? You want me to thumb my nose at her? And there's something else, too. I was away at college for three years, and every time I really needed money, Mom sent it. Where do you think Mom found five hundred dollars every semester for books and fees?"

David considered this. "You think it was from Mrs. Whiting?"

"She didn't get it from Max. Who else was there?"

"I don't know," David admitted, "but at least we're finally talking about the right person."

"What's that supposed to mean?"

"It means when you said you owed her, that's who I thought you were talking about. Mom. If you were saying you owed *her*, that would have made some sense."

"I don't need you to tell me how much I owe her, David."

"Yeah? Well, there's only one way to pay off that debt, big brother. And I'm sorry, but you *do* need reminding about the way things were. Mom never wanted you to come back. Your getting out of here was her life's work. You know that better than I do. If she borrowed money from Mrs. Whiting, you can bet she paid it back in full. Services rendered. She practically raised that woman's daughter. And if she knew you'd ended up forty-two and running the Empire Grill, she'd turn over in her grave."

Miles rubbed his temples with his thumbs, feeling the first aura of a headache coming on. "I'm sure you're right that she'd be disappointed," he conceded, knowing too that "disappointed" was too lame a word for it. "Brokenhearted" was more like it. "No doubt I've shamed her. I feel like I have, believe me. But the one thing I don't think I'd have to explain to Grace Roby is that a kid comes first. Maybe I was wrong to come back, but I've got Tick now, and I can't put her in jeopardy. I won't."

"And you imagine I would? You think I'd advise you to?"

"Isn't that what you're doing? Last week you were all for that bookstore I can't afford on Martha's Vineyard. Now you want me to make Mrs. Whiting my enemy by going into business with Bea. Have you ever looked at that kitchen? Do you have any idea how much fixing it up would cost?"

"Between us we could—"

Miles couldn't listen. "David, if you want to go into business with Bea, then *go*. I give you my blessing."

His brother nodded slowly, as if this whole conversation had already taken place numerous times and there were just one or two minor details he'd failed to memorize. "All right," he said finally. "Since I've already pissed you off, I'll try this one more time and then give up. I *know* you've got Tick, Miles. And I know you're in a tight spot. In fact, I'm even more worried about the spot you're in than you are, because it's worse than you think. What I'm trying to say is that it isn't going to get any better. That woman's got you on a treadmill, Miles. You're running so hard all the time just to keep up that you can't see it. It's what Mom feared. It's what she knew would happen if you—"

"Tell me something," Miles interrupted. "Why do you hate Mrs. Whiting so much?"

"Look," he said, "it's not a question of hating her. You think she'll give you the restaurant like she promised, and then you'll sell it and get out, right?" When Miles didn't say anything, he continued, "Except Mrs. Whiting isn't dying, Miles. You know what she's doing instead? She's living. In Italy for a month when it suits her. In Florida during the winter. Santa Fe in the late spring. You're the one that's dying, Miles, a day at a time. Do you have any idea how old Mrs. Whiting's mother was when she died?"

"None," Miles confessed.

"That's because she's still alive," David told him. "She's in a nursing home in Fairhaven, in her nineties. If Mrs. Whiting lives that long, you'll be sixty-five when you inherit the grill. That's *if* she gives it to you. And that's not even the worst part, Miles. You claim you're sticking it out for Tick, but do you know what that kid's going to be if you aren't careful? She'll be the next manager of the Empire Grill."

"Over my dead body," Miles said.

His brother got to his feet and smiled, clearly having seen this coming. "Good. Now we've come full circle. That's what Mom always said about you."

David tossed his empty soda bottle into the trash can by the door. "Look, I'm sorry I said anything. I should go home. I already know how this is going to end."

For a moment Miles thought that he was referring to their discussion, but then he realized that David probably meant the ball game. The Sox held a slender one-run lead in the seventh, and history, both recent and not so recent, suggested it wouldn't hold up. September was a bad month for New England baseball fans. You could spend most of it searching in vain for reasons you were so optimistic back in April. Next April was when you'd remember them.

"When's Buster coming back?" David wondered, referring to the grill's other fry cook, who'd commenced his bender the day Miles returned from Martha's Vineyard.

Miles doubted his brother really cared about Buster. David was just anxious that they not part angry. His question was designed to restore the usual equilibrium. "I'll see if I can hunt him down tomorrow."

"We're going to need another waitress and busboy, too."

"I know. I'll get on it."

"Okay," David said, starting out, then stopping, one hand on the doorknob. "What was Janine all upset about tonight?"

"I don't know," Miles said, meeting his brother's eye. The simple truth. "Cold feet, probably."

David nodded. "I should hope. Given the man she intends to marry, she ought to be cold all the way up to her barrettes."

"I don't think women wear those anymore, do they?" It'd been so long since Miles had loosened a woman's hair that he'd lost track.

"Funny thing, though," David said, still standing in the doorway.

Miles studied him, dead certain that what came next would not be funny in the least.

"The two of you sitting there in that booth tonight looked more like lovers than you ever did when you were married."

"Funny?" Miles said sadly. "That's hilarious."

Mrs. Whiting's refrain, he realized.

David was all the way down the back stairs when Miles remembered something and hurried after him. His brother was backing his pickup out of his space behind the restaurant, a complicated maneuver for a man with only one good arm, when Miles rapped on the window.

"Listen," Miles began, "tell me to mind my own business . . ."

"Okay, I will," David promised.

"Are you growing marijuana out there at the lake?"

His brother snorted. "Why, Miles? Do you want some?"

Miles didn't see why this seemed so damned funny, but he let it go. "Jimmy Minty thinks you are, is the reason I mention it."

"Jimmy Minty *thinks*?"

"Apparently."

"Why tell you?"

"He characterized it as a friendly warning, since we're all old friends. I sort of told him to fuck off. I also told him I didn't think you were."

David nodded. "You see him, tell him I said thanks for the tip."

When his brother started rolling the window back up, Miles rapped on it again. "You didn't answer my question," he said. "*Are* you growing marijuana out there?"

David smiled. "Mind your own business."

"You always talk about Mom as if I was the only one she had plans for. That's not true, you know."

David nodded. "I know exactly what she wanted me to do, because she told me before she died."

Something in Miles sensed a trap, but since it was his brother who'd set it, he decided to walk right in. "What was that?"

"Look after your brother," David said, backing out.

"Wно's тнат just came in?" Max Roby wanted to know when he felt the air change in the tavern. Sitting at the far end of the bar, he heard the front door swing shut with a dull thud. Whoever it was had stopped at the cigarette machine, a promising sign. Max leaned back on his stool, squinting across the dark room, trying to make out who it was. Since he'd turned seventy, his eyes weren't as good as they used to be. Fortunately, he could still climb like a monkey.

"It's Horace Weymouth," Bea Majeski told him from behind the bar. "Leave him alone."

Bea was just now pondering whether to close Callahan's for the night. It was going on midnight, and her only customer was Max Roby, who you couldn't really call a customer because he perpetually hovered at his hundred-dollar credit limit. Truth be told, most of Bea's customers were the same. They'd pay down their tabs by ten or twenty bucks in the afternoon, then drink them back up to a hundred by closing time. Unless she got lucky and one of them handed her a twenty and keeled over on the spot, every goddamn one of these deadbeats was going to die owing her a hundred dollars. Even the stiff that had handed her the twenty would owe her eighty. About the only trade Callahan's got anymore was from the Empire Towers, the subsidized senior citizens' housing facility down the block. First of the month, after they got their checks, the geezers would stream in. They'd drink old-fashioneds and sidecars for a few days, but by the tenth or so, they'd have blown their booze allotment and Bea wouldn't see any of them again until the first. Except for Max Roby. He also lived over at

David nodded. "I know exactly what she wanted me to do, because she told me before she died."

Something in Miles sensed a trap, but since it was his brother who'd set it, he decided to walk right in. "What was that?"

"Look after your brother," David said, backing out.

"WHO'S THAT just came in?" Max Roby wanted to know when he felt the air change in the tavern. Sitting at the far end of the bar, he heard the front door swing shut with a dull thud. Whoever it was had stopped at the cigarette machine, a promising sign. Max leaned back on his stool, squinting across the dark room, trying to make out who it was. Since he'd turned seventy, his eyes weren't as good as they used to be. Fortunately, he could still climb like a monkey.

"It's Horace Weymouth," Bea Majeski told him from behind the bar. "Leave him alone."

Bea was just now pondering whether to close Callahan's for the night. It was going on midnight, and her only customer was Max Roby, who you couldn't really call a customer because he perpetually hovered at his hundred-dollar credit limit. Truth be told, most of Bea's customers were the same. They'd pay down their tabs by ten or twenty bucks in the afternoon, then drink them back up to a hundred by closing time. Unless she got lucky and one of them handed her a twenty and keeled over on the spot, every goddamn one of these deadbeats was going to die owing her a hundred dollars. Even the stiff that had handed her the twenty would owe her eighty. About the only trade Callahan's got anymore was from the Empire Towers, the subsidized senior citizens' housing facility down the block. First of the month, after they got their checks, the geezers would stream in. They'd drink old-fashioneds and sidecars for a few days, but by the tenth or so, they'd have blown their booze allotment and Bea wouldn't see any of them again until the first. Except for Max Roby. He also lived over at the Towers, but he turned up regardless. At least the geezers didn't start fights, she told herself. Again, except for Max Roby.

"In fact," Bea told him now, suspecting that her previous instructions might be interpreted too narrowly, "leave everybody alone."

"Invite him down here," Max suggested. "I could use some company."

Bea glared at him. "What'd I *just* say?"

"How's that bothering anybody? I like Horace."

"Me too," Bea said, studying him in the entryway hunched over the cigarette machine, madly pulling at the levers now. He'd clearly abandoned his own brand for whatever the machine might deign to give him. "Which is why I told you to leave him alone. A man ought to be able to come in here without you bumming cigarettes and draft beers."

Out in the entryway, the machine surrendered a pack of some brand or other, which Horace bent down to scoop out of the trough. When he raised up again and turned toward the bar, he caught sight of Max, the only customer, seated at the far end, where Bea always parked him because he smelled rancid and was a pain in the ass. This sight occasioned a small hitch in Horace's giddy-up, a split second's hesitation, during which a man might consider his options. Like leaving. Other men had been known to turn promptly on their heels upon spying Max, but all his life Horace had been victimized by his own good manners. A reporter for the *Empire Gazette* for going on thirty years, he'd seen humanity from every angle. Most people, he concluded, were selfish, greedy, unprincipled, venal, utterly irredeemable shit-eaters, but he'd also observed that these same people were highly sensitive to criticism. Max Roby was an exception, but Horace nonetheless couldn't bring himself to hurt the man's feelings. Which meant he also couldn't plop down at the opposite end of the bar. That strategy wouldn't work anyway, since the exact same conversation would ensue, with Max shouting it.

"What'd it give you this time?" Max said in an idly curious tone when Horace slid onto a nearby stool, leaving one between them as a buffer zone, however inadequate. Horace tried to imagine the situation whereby someone would come in and fill *that* vacancy. It'd have to be a stranger. A blind stranger. No sense of smell, either.

"Chesterfields," Horace said, examining the pack before placing it on the bar alongside a twenty-dollar bill. Bea poured him a draft and slid an ashtray in front of him, leaving the twenty where it was, for now. "You want one, Max?"

"Sure," he said, leaning over to snatch the pack, then deftly peeling off its slender ribbon, thumbing up its flip top, discarding the foil and removing two cigarettes.

Horace noted that Max had taken two, not one, but said nothing, just as Max had known he wouldn't. "You might as well draw one for my friend here," he told Bea. "He's got that thirsty look."

Bea did not approve of Horace's generosity, but she complied with his request. "Working late?" she asked.

Horace nodded. Tonight had been a beaut. For starters he'd had to cover the school board meeting in Fairhaven, one of his least favorite assignments; this one had progressed rapidly from civil to uncivil to angry to plain insulting, stopping just short of fisticuffs. Then, on the way home, his car had broken down on a seldom-used back road out by the old landfill. There was only one house within a radius of about a mile, and Horace, hoping to use the phone to call for a tow, had walked up the long dirt driveway and there, around back of the dark old house, had secretly witnessed something that had rattled him to the core, something that went far beyond the selfish, greedy, unprincipled, venal, utterly irredeemable shit-eating behavior he was used to and sent him stealing back out to the road, as if he himself and not that sad, alarming boy had been the guilty party. As he walked nearly three miles into town, what he'd witnessed was with him every step, and it made him glad of companionship now, even if one of his companions was Max Roby.

"You should get that thing removed," Max suggested, glancing at the fibroid cyst on Horace's forehead.

"What thing?" Horace said, his standard reply to such comments, which were more frequent than anyone would imagine.

"I'm always afraid it'll explode when I'm talking to you," Max said, draining half of his beer in one sudden motion. It hadn't been Max's intention to gulp so much, but he'd been perched there on his barstool, dry, for a hell of a while. A bar could become a desert when you were broke, its beer spigots a mirage. When you finally arrived at the oasis you could tell yourself not to drink too deeply, but a body parched so long by the desert sand has its own needs, its own devices, and Max was just glad his body hadn't demanded the whole glass Horace had bought him. The idea now was to be patient and adjust himself to the pace of the man he hoped to continue drinking with. If he tried to push Horace by draining his own glass too quickly, the other man would feel pressured and leave, then Max would be smack-dab in the middle of